HER VIGILANT
SEAL

MIDNIGHT DELTA SERIES
BOOK ONE

CAITLYN O'LEARY

To all of our men and women who have served.

HER VIGILANT SEAL

A Heart of Gold
Sophia Anderson takes care of everyone but herself. She will stop at nothing to keep her family safe. When she goes searching for her runaway little brother in a bad part of town, she becomes the one in need of rescue.

A White Knight
Navy SEAL, Mason Gault, faced many dangers while in the line of duty. No matter how bad a mission has gone, he finds solace in three things: His family, friends and the waves of the Pacific. When he hears a woman's screams for help, he charges in to save her without a second thought.

A Dangerous Love
Sophia is burdened with scars from her past. Mason understands that empowering her spirit is just as important as protecting her well-being. As their love and passion soars, so do threats against her. Can Mason continue to be the compassionate white knight that she needs, while ensuring her safety?

CHAPTER ONE

January...

"Lieutenant, you gotta let me carry him, you're wounded."

"I'm fine. It's just a scratch." Mason knew he wasn't holding his team back. Even while holding Jones' body with a knife wound in his forearm, he could keep up with the rest of them.

"We're still six miles to the shoreline you can't keep up at this pace." Mason couldn't believe Drake was serious as blood seeped through his own tourniquet. *Stubborn fool.*

"Drake, when it becomes a problem I'll make a different decision, until then, I'm carrying him." They'd taken down their target. Six of Mason's team of eight men had been together for over two years and Lou Jones was their first casualty. He hadn't followed orders and it cost him his life. Didn't matter, it was on Mason's watch and he'd be damned if he wasn't going to be the one to carry him home.

"Let me take him Mason, just for fifteen minutes." He looked over at his second-in-command. Drake was out of his mind, he'd actually taken a worse hit to his thigh, and he was volunteering to carry a dead man.

"Your job is to keep from bleeding to death," Mason gritted out.

"I've cut myself worse while shaving." Drake flashed him a grin.

"You shave your legs? Is there something you want to tell me?"

He laughed, just as Mason known he would.

"Somebody set us up, they knew we were coming." Mason was beginning to feel the burn from the long run and carrying his load.

"That's my take too," Drake agreed. "Seriously, let me take Jones' body, I'm good for a half a mile, and you need to fall back a bit and check on the others." Drake was right, Mason needed to check on the other six SEALs. They made the transfer and he slowed his pace so he could mix in with the other men.

"I'm sorry I suggested you leave Jones behind earlier. I was wrong," Ensign Steve Fairfax said. All of them were whispering as they ran through the jungle. Mason still had trouble believing Fairfax had first suggested it when his friend had been shot. All of the rest of Midnight Delta had been dumfounded.

"Yes you were," Mason concurred. Steve joined them a few months ago, and he'd been Lou's best friend. Neither man had followed orders. Steve wouldn't be with the team after this op. Mason felt a hand clap his shoulder and knew it was Petty Officer Larry Clark.

"Mase, you okay?" His voice too low for Steve to hear.

"I'm good, what about you?" Mason saw Larry had been grazed. Darius, the team's medic, must have applied a tourniquet while they were at the compound where the raid went down.

"I'm fine." Larry grinned. "Nothing a little time in the hospital won't take care of." Mason shook his head. Larry was currently dating two different nurses at the naval base.

"If you ever get caught this injury will seem like a walk in the park."

"I keep hoping neither of them will want to give me up, so we'll have to settle for a ménage." He winked.

"I want to live in the wonderland that is your mind for just one hour. It must be nice to still believe in fairytales."

"What's nice is all the *tail*."

Mason looked at his friend in amazement and Larry gave him a shit eating grin.

Mason reached Drake and took Jones' body again. Five hundred yards before they were going to break through the jungle to the beach everyone halted. Drake went ahead to the waiting Zodiac to make sure things were clear. A half hour later he came back shaking his head, and they huddled around him.

"We've got tangos three in the trees waiting to pick us off, and we have four at our boat."

"We're going to have to take them all at the same time," Mason said. He and Drake outlined their plans. "No matter what happens we have to shoot at precisely five minutes after the hour. Remember, one SEAL, one shot, it's a piece of cake."

They spread out according to their assigned targets. Mason looked at his watch, in five more minutes they would be in position.

Mason heard the crack of someone stepping on a tree branch and then a shot rang out. *Dammit!* He knew his men weren't in position. Mason already had his bogey targeted so he took him out and ran forward as fast as he could to the next tree. The man was still taking shots at the SEALs on the ground. Mason aimed carefully and took him out. The third man in the trees was at least a hundred yards to his left so he headed for the beach confident Finn would take him. Almost to the tree line that opened to the shore, he found Larry's body covering Steve Fairfax. Fairfax was hit in the chest, and he was critical but trying to talk.

"Save your breath, son," Mason said calmly, trying to soothe the young man.

"I'm sorry, Lieutenant." Tears welled up in his eyes.

"Not your fault."

"I shot too soon. Thought..." He gasped for breath.

"Stop talking that's an order. I need you to save your strength." He pushed Larry's body back on top of Steve's chest, knowing it was the best option to compress the wound. He couldn't shout for Darius, not yet knowing if the coast was clear or if the medic was under fire.

Mason crept towards the beach hoping the lack of gunfire was a good thing. Finally he heard someone yelling his name.

"I'm here!" Mason yelled. "I need Darius." He pushed through the trees. The rest of the team were standing or bending over, but at least on they were all on their feet. Darius rushed forward.

"Where are you hurt, Lieutenant?"

"Not me it's Fairfax." Mason saw Darius' lip curl before he masked his feelings.

"Show me." Mason took him to the spot he'd left Fairfax. They moved Larry, and Darius went to work on the ensign.

"Mason, it doesn't look good. We've got to get him on the boat fast." When Mason looked up, he saw the rest of the team was already there. They picked up Larry's and Lou's bodies. Drake helped him and Darius carry Fairfax to the Zodiac.

Finn was the last one in, he was carrying Larry, but he slipped and they both went into the water. Mason went over, plummeting into cold ocean water through the slick of warm red blood. He forced himself to get Larry's body back onto the boat.

"Mason, are you listening to me?" His arm was being yanked, and he saw Darius ripping the arm of his shirt.

"What? It's nothing. How's Drake?" Mason looked around the boat. There were three bodies, how in the hell had that happened?

"Mase, you need to listen to me. You're going into shock."

"I'm fine, Dare. Go look at Drake."

"I already did. He wasn't in the water. He didn't rip his wound open even more lifting two hundred pounds into a boat."

Larry. How was the team going to function without Larry?

"I'm doing great. I lived, Dare. I lived. Just tie it off, and we'll wait 'til we meet up with our ride, okay?" Mason looked his friend in the eye. Darius must have seen something, because he quit talking and just bandaged him up and left him leaning against the side of the boat, lost in sorrow and regret.

Chapter Two

February...

Mason Gault paddled on this board in the Pacific Ocean, focusing on the pristine water of Moonlight Beach. He felt the swell, and hopped up onto his surfboard in a crouch like he was sixteen again. He stayed in place waiting, swaying, and then he was off like a rocket, sailing upwards, catching the mass of energy taking him into white and shiny water. He rode the wave for seconds, minutes, or maybe hours. Time had no meaning. Finally he went down and laughed as he bobbed back up through the surf, seeing the dawn sky.

He surfed for a long while. He had come alone, like he had every day for the last week. He was still trying to get his head on straight from his last mission. He was doing all of the things the Navy thought was *good* for him, but nothing was better than these moments in the waves. Here he could breathe. Here there were no bullets, no blood, and no death.

* * *

Sophia remembered when she had a sunny outlook on life. That's why she came to Moonlight Beach at sunrise. She hoped she would get the spark to come back. Oh, she faked it for her mother, but she wanted to be that little girl again for real, the one who believed the world was a good place. She tasted the noodles in her cup. They weren't warm anymore. She pulled the thermos of hot water out of her backpack and poured a little more into the Styrofoam container. She needed the hot meal, so she better eat it, after all breakfast was the most important meal of the day.

Sitting on top of the picnic table, she sat on her pink blanket and huddled in her over-sized red sweater. Eating her noodles, she watched the surfer as the sun came up, wishing for things that weren't meant to be. It was the fifth day in a row she and the surfer had been here. There were plenty of other surfers, but none seemed as frantic, as lost, or as lonely as she was. The fact she was projecting her emotions on to him just proved how close she was to losing it.

Looking into her empty cup of noodles, Sophia realized she was still hungry. She smiled, it was her second smile of the morning. Of course she was still hungry, her stomach was constantly growling for three months now. But her mom's medicine was more important than food. She looked to see if she could get a third smile before she left. Yes, there was a God! The surfer was coming out of the water carrying his board. She'd yet to see him with the wet suit unzipped, imagine how hungry she'd be then?

Sophia hastily put the remnants of her meal into her backpack, folded the blanket, and headed for the parking lot. This little detour to Moonlight Beach in Encinitas ate up an extra buck fifty in gas, but the way it soothed her soul was worth it, wasn't it? She headed towards the compounding pharmacy to pick-up her Mom's medicine, then went on towards the food pantry in San Clemente.

"Sophia, you look pretty today." Mr. DeLuca smiled at her. He pointed her to the smallest box of bananas that must have just come in. He grabbed the larger box and took them to the back area of the pantry.

"Thank you, Tony, and you look very handsome today," she said to the older man as she started to sort the fruit. Unfortunately only one third of the bananas would be fresh enough to go into the children's lunches.

"It must be the way I did my hair," he said as he smoothed his hand over his bald head.

"Quit flirting with Sophia, otherwise she might take you up on it and find out you stopped delivering twenty years ago," Mrs. DeLuca called from the bread aisle. Sophia snorted. This was why she came here and donated her time. She originally started coming because they needed the food for her mother and younger brother, but after her mother became so ill and her brother got taken away this had become her refuge. She still brought home food from the pantry to feed herself and her mother, but at odd hours when her mother was resting she could now donate her time in return.

She secretly loved that Tony always called her pretty. She knew she really wasn't. Compared to most girls in Southern California she was plain. Oh, her long blonde hair was nice, but her face had a smattering of freckles, her nose was too wide, and her green eyes would have looked better if she was a brunette. Even at twenty-two she still didn't have much of a figure. Now that she'd lost weight she kind of looked like a board. But Tony made her feel special.

"Have you had breakfast, Bella?" he asked bluntly.

"Yes."

"No she hasn't, Tony. She's tinier than last month, make her eat something," Frannie bellowed from the other room.

"I'm fine. I had breakfast." She'd had the cup of noodles at the beach, but being at home in the trailer with her mother so sick, made her lose her appetite.

"Enough!" Mrs. DeLuca pounded her way to the kitchen where Sophia was sorting through the rotten fruit.

"Come with me right now." Mrs. DeLuca, who was twice Sophia's normal size, grabbed her upper arm and looked her in the eye. "I will drag you out of here if you make me. Are you coming willingly or will you make me force you?"

Shocked, Sophia finally said, "Willingly."

Five doors down was one of the busiest diners in town and the proof was in the fact that at barely seven a.m. there wasn't a seat available.

"We don't have time and there's no place to sit." Sophia tugged her arm trying to get Frannie DeLuca to let her loose.

"Margie," Frannie yelled out. A woman came out from the back of the diner and hugged Frannie.

"Hello, who have we here?" the woman said looking Sophia up and down.

"This is Sophia, the girl I've been telling you about. The one whose mama is so sick. She needs some breakfast." Margie looked around the diner, she must have noticed the two men who were nursing cups of coffee because she went over and whispered something. They got up and smiled at Frannie as they made their way to the register.

"A table just opened up." The customers who had been waiting in line started to groan, grumble, and protest.

"You just keep a civil tone. I've always done right by you. This is Frannie from the food pantry, she's taking a break from packing lunches for the kids who need 'em. She has to get back quick. So you can all quit your whining." Margie cast an evil eye at the crowd and some of them chuckled, most just quieted down.

After they were seated, Margie popped menus in their hands and said she would be back in a moment to take their orders.

"I can't let you pay for my breakfast," Sophia protested.

"I can afford to buy you breakfast so pick whatever you want on the menu." Sophia knew Tony and Frannie lived on Social Security and really didn't want to take her money.

"I can afford it. Now order what you want." When Margie came back she placed her order, and Frannie added a cinnamon roll and a large glass of orange juice.

"Honey, in the five months you've been coming to the food pantry, you've lost a lot of weight." Frannie's tone was blunt, but she gave Sophia's hand a motherly pat.

"I've always wanted to be this size. Who knew the being broke diet was so damn easy." Sophia loved Frannie's laugh.

"Tell me what's going on with your mother and your brother, Billy." Sophia smiled at Frannie's tone. There were no questions from Frannie DeLuca, she expected to be kept up-to-date like a kindly aunt. She made Sophia feel good.

"The nurse that came over yesterday said it would be any-time now. I feel guilty coming to the pantry, but it feels wrong staying in the little trailer, basically sitting on top of her and waiting for her to die, you know?" Sophia's voice broke. For the past two years she'd been taking care of her mother, who was slowly dying from lung cancer. In the last few months it had gotten much worse when the cancer metastasized to her brain. Her mother didn't have much longer to live.

"Does she recognize you?"

"Occasionally. She did last week. Most of the time she calls me mom and asks about her dad and brothers." Sophia pulled at her hair and her voice trembled as she explained.

"What are your plans regarding Billy after she passes?" Frannie held Sophia's hand tighter.

"I want Billy to come and live with me. We're family. He likes the Bards, but he's told me again and again he wants to live with me. After she dies, I'll need to get a job and a place to live that DHCS will find suitable and then petition for custody." Sophia was now pulling and twirling her hair with one hand, as she held onto Frannie's hand with the other.

Margie placed the food in front of her, and even though she'd been so hungry, she couldn't seem to bring herself to eat.

"I'm so sorry about your mama honey. But after she passes you'll be able to take in Billy and that'll be a blessing," Margie said kindly as she patted her shoulder.

Sophia looked at the icing on the cinnamon roll and felt like she was going to throw up. It was all too much. She didn't know what she was going to do. As soon as her mother passed away the pension would stop. Sophia needed a job like yesterday, but she couldn't leave her mom, but no more than a month after she died she wouldn't have a place to stay.

Dammit, how had this happened? She'd been going to college, had scholarships, and a part-time internship. She'd even had a boy who she thought loved her. She'd been normal. She'd been making it. It all stopped when her mom needed full-time care. Now she needed to find a job fast. She'd already started to contact local women's shelters, so she'd have a place to stay until she could afford first and last month's rent. She didn't know if she would be able to get a good enough job to be able to pay for an apartment that would pass muster with DCHS, so Billy might have to continue in foster care. What was she going to do?

"Honey, you have to eat."

"Don't you like my food?" Margie asked as she topped off Frannie's coffee.

To Sophia's absolute horror, Frannie explained Sophia's circumstances to the owner of the diner. She had no idea Frannie knew every little detail, and here she was gossiping about it. Sophia wanted to crawl underneath the table.

"I am so sorry to hear that. I remember when my mom died, it damn near broke my heart," Margie said as she sat down next to Frannie. "But perhaps you could do me a hell of a favor when the time comes."

Sophia looked at the older woman in confusion. She was still considering sinking beneath the table, except Frannie was looking at her with love.

"What kind of favor do you need?" Frannie asked.

"I need someone to start opening the diner for me. I promised my son I would move in with him and his wife, and stop the early morning openings. I've been looking for someone reliable that I could have takeover the apartment above the diner, start the morning baking, and then open." Margie stopped and turned red in the face.

"What Margie?" Frannie asked. "What the hell are you doing looking like you swallowed a golf ball? It sounds like a perfect set up for Sophia."

"Do you know how to bake?" Margie blurted out. Sophia nodded and Frannie laughed.

"I used to bake all the time." Sophia's eyes lit up.

"Well all right then. When the time comes, come talk to me and we'll set it all up." Margie nodded her head and smiled.

"Look Margie, I couldn't possibly. I don't even know your last name. I haven't filled out an application. This just isn't right." Sophia was appalled the woman was making such a big decision after barely knowing her an hour.

"It's right. I believe God sends us who and what we need when we need it. The apartment over the shop probably won't be good enough to get custody of your brother, but it should be a start to get you back on your feet."

"I can't," Sophia said, but Margie smiled and left the table.

"Well that went well," Frannie said.

"She can't possibly be serious," she said looking at her friend in amazement.

"Oh, she's serious." Frannie chuckled.

CHAPTER THREE

Five Months Later...

Downtown San Diego at three in the morning was scary and Sophia couldn't imagine how frightening it would be for a twelve year old boy. The police were on the lookout for Billy, but she had to try to find him herself. This was the fourth time he'd run away. Last time he had been found near Encanto Park so she thought looking for him there made sense.

She'd been walking up and down the streets and checking out the different hidey-holes. Last time she'd found Billy huddled in an alley with a homeless man. He wasn't in the same place so she looked even further afield. She had brought a flashlight with her and turned it toward the sounds coming from a Mercedes parked on an empty industrial street.

The back door was open and a man was standing beside it. She heard the sound again and realized it was a girl's voice crying the word, "No." As she got closer she saw another man with his pants around his thighs bent over the backseat of the car. It was obvious what he was doing.

"Come on hurry up, I want my turn," the man who was standing said. Sophia grabbed her phone out of the front pocket of her hoodie just as the man looked up and saw her.

"Well hello, nice of you to join the party." He leered.

She got the phone unlocked as the man rushed her and batted the phone to the ground. She heard the girl scream again. Ducking her head around the side of the man in front of her she yelled, "Quit hurting her."

"She's on the clock. We paid for her time. She knew what she was getting into." The man grabbed Sophia by her hair and dragged her over to the car. The girl was sobbing. Sophia screamed for all she was worth. The man backhanded her, and she fell onto the hood of the car hitting her ribs hard against the steel.

"Look at me, bitch." Sophia looked at the man who held her hair, he had crooked teeth and an evil smile. "This is nice we each get one." Sophia opened her mouth to scream again but he put his hands around her neck and started to squeeze.

"Scream again and I'll strangle you." Sophia gasped for air when he let go and he laughed. She heard the girl crying even harder.

"Please let her go," Sophia begged. Suddenly the second man was beside the first.

"What will you do if I stop? Will you cooperate?" He was holding his pants up with one hand and a broken beer bottle in the other. He turned to the man who kept her shoved on to the car. "I like them when they'll do what I want, and you know the things I want." He and his friend laughed uproariously.

"Yes, anything. Just don't hurt her anymore." Sophia meant it. She could survive this, just as long as they didn't hurt the poor girl anymore. The girl was sobbing quietly.

"Now that sounds like fun. I vote for a little two on one action. I like 'em willing. The other one might be a pro but she sure isn't acting like one."

Sophia hoped the girl would take this opportunity to run. Sophia forced her hand into the front pocket of her hoodie and pulled out the can of mace. She held up the can of pepper spray and depressed the trigger.

"Bitch!" The first man screamed as it hit his eyes and the second man grabbed her arm and held it backwards. "On your knees bitch or I'll break your arm." Out of the corner of her eye she finally saw the girl scrambling away. *Thank God.*

She was pushed down to the ground and two sets of hands worked to pull her hoodie over her head. The second man used the jagged edges of the beer bottle to cut her bra off. Sophia kept kicking, until one of the two men sat on her legs.

"Give me the bottle," the first man said. "She needs to pay," he said as he rubbed at his streaming eyes. He held his hand over her mouth, and then pressed the tip of the bottle into her flesh cutting a line down her shoulder.

"There, that won't interfere with the good parts." He laughed. Fire burst down her arm from her shoulder. She felt blood pulsing from the cut, hurting with each heartbeat.

"Pay attention. We're going to teach you some tricks." Evil gleamed in his eyes.

Her breasts were groped and twisted. Then she heard a girl yell, "Over there, please mister, you've got to help her."

The man holding her turned around at the sound of the other girl's loud voice. Distracted, he let go of her mouth and Sophia screamed at the top of her lungs. A fist slammed into the side of her head and face. She saw a shadow above the two men. *Oh God, not a third one.* And then she heard one of the two men screech as he was pulled off of her.

"Use my phone and call 911," the shadow yelled to the girl.

That was the last thing Sophia heard as pain engulfed her.

* * *

"Ah hell, it's Sophia," the cop said as he crouched next to the woman in Mason's arms.

"How do you know her?" Mason's head jerked up and he eyed the cop.

"She's been looking for her brother again. He keeps running away from his foster home. She's been searching for him the last four nights. I told her it wasn't safe." Mason looked down at the unconscious woman and agreed with the patrolman's assessment.

"How much longer before the ambulance arrives?" Mason clipped out the question.

"How bad is she? What happened?" The cop nodded to where Mason's jacket was covering Sophia's torso.

"They just got her top off, but they cut her pretty badly on the arm. I've got her bandaged and most of the bleeding stopped. She's going to need a shit-load of stitches. What's the ETA on the ambulance?" Mason shifted her gently as he again gave the cop a penetrating stare.

"It's about fifteen more minutes. There was a bad pile-up on the Five Freeway with fatalities. You did good work tonight. You military?" the cop asked as he assessed Mason.

"SEAL."

"I was Navy too," the cop said. "You okay with her while I work on getting these two assholes taken care of?" The cop nodded towards the two thugs who were sitting handcuffed in the alley and being looked after by his partner.

"I've got her." Mason looked down at Sophia again ensuring she was okay. "What about the girl who made the call?"

"What girl?" the cop asked.

Mason looked around and realized the girl and his phone were long gone.

"There was another girl who looked like she'd been beaten too. She got me to come over here to help." Mason gave the information like he was reporting to his commander.

"She must have taken off after she called for help," the officer said.

"Oh no," came the soft words. Mason looked down and saw green eyes clouded with worry looking up at him.

"What? Did you say something Sophia?" he asked.

"The girl is gone? She's hurt." It was hard to understand her through her bruised mouth.

"Settle honey, you're hurt. You need to stay calm and rest until the ambulance comes." Mason watched as she struggled to get up, and then cried out in pain. She collapsed against him. Fuck, it had to be her shoulder. He'd already taken off his shirt and used it as a bandage and a tourniquet earlier. He eased back the leather jacket that he had placed over her to see if it had come loose.

"Don't move again, okay Sophia." *God, when will the ambulance get here?*

"You've got to find the girl I think they cut her too. I've got to get up, I need to look for Billy. Please don't hold me down. I need to get up, let me up," she damn near screamed the last few words. Mason realized she was delirious. The cop looked over at him and he shook his head.

"Sophia, my name is Mason. We're going to get you to the hospital. Do you understand me, honey?" He waited to see if she was tracking. She finally nodded. "Good, after they're done taking care of you, you can come look for Billy again." She relaxed a little, and he relaxed a little as well.

"And the girl? Can I look for the girl too?" she begged him with big eyes.

"Yes, you can look for the girl too." He stroked the hair from her forehead.

"Do you promise Mason?" She tried to lift her arm to grab the front of his jacket and let out a small shriek of pain. "Why does it hurt?" He saw her start to tremble and wrapped his jacket closer around her ensuring it was snug so she couldn't move her arms any longer.

"Are you warm now?"

"Yes. Will I be able to go to work and then look for Billy tomorrow?" It took a moment for him to understand her, and when he did it took him a few seconds to formulate a response other than 'Hell No'.

"I think you're going to be in the hospital for at least a couple of days."

"No, I hate hospitals, don't make me go to the hospital." He watched as tears dripped down her temples into her silky blonde hair.

"Honey, you have to go you've been injured. A doctor has to help you." She was trembling so bad he was worried she was going into shock.

"I can't afford a hospital. Can you take me home?" God, she was breaking his heart.

"Let's see what the doctor says first."

Mason heard the siren and Sophia must have heard it too. Somehow she pushed off the heavy leather coat. "No, no ambulance, no hospital. I have to find Billy." She tried getting up one last time and groaned as she put pressure on her cut shoulder.

"You've got to stay still." He couldn't believe the compassion this woman had, here she was bleeding and bruised, almost raped, and her entire concern was for her brother and the other girl. She was beautiful inside and out.

Just then she gripped her head where he saw a large bruise and lump forming. He saw her green eyes begin to glaze over. "Honey, stay with me." He brushed his fingers tenderly along her cheek willing her to stay awake.

"Mason's a nice name," her words were slurred.

Just as the EMTs arrived she passed out.

CHAPTER FOUR

A second patrol car picked up the two perps. Mason asked the cop who knew Sophia if he could catch a ride with him to the hospital.

"Sure. Stan already took your statement?" Mason nodded. "You just want to check on Sophia, right?"

"Yeah. I'd drive myself, but my car is over at my house in Lincoln Park. I was out for a walk."

"What the hell are you doing walking in this neighborhood?" Officer Duffy asked giving him an incredulous look. Mason rubbed the back of his neck.

"Look. You and I both know there are a lot of homeless vets out here. I bring them some sandwiches on some nights when I can't sleep. Sometimes I talk to them." Duffy didn't say anything for a while, just looked at him and finally nodded.

"Lucky for Sophia." He clapped Mason on his shoulder. "Yeah, I'll drive you over."

The ER was a mess. Duffy was able to get them into the back where they finally found Sophia in a curtained area. She was holding Mason's shirt to her shoulder and wearing Mason's coat. He was wearing a spare T-Shirt the officer had in his duffel bag.

As soon as they spotted her the cop veered off and went to find someone to see about her treatment. Officer Duffy brought back an intern.

"I'm sorry, Ms. Anderson, we've had some critically injured people come in with the car wreck on the Five Freeway. Let's get you situated where I can take a look at your wound, shall we?" Mason was liking Duffy more and more.

"Doc, I'm going to have to ask her some questions," Duffy said apologetically.

"After I get her settled," the doctor said. He shooed Mason and Duffy away, and then a few minutes later opened the curtain. Sophia was lying down. She looked alert but in pain.

"Who are you?" the doctor asked Mason.

"I'm her fiancée," Mason lied easily. Sophia's eyes fluttered open, but then she closed them again. Officer Duffy went to the head of the bed.

"Sophia, are you up for answering a couple of questions?" the cop asked her.

"Doctor Jefferson? We need you STAT," a nurse called.

The doctor looked at Sophia, and pulled some gauze and handed it to Mason. "Keep that on her arm and apply steady pressure. I'll be back as soon as I can."

"Officer Duffy?" Sophia whispered.

"What Sophia."

"Get a nurse," Sophia sounded desperate.

Duffy looked around, and it was clear everyone was really busy.

"No one's available is there anything I can help you with?" he asked kindly.

"I'm going to be sick." Duffy found a pan underneath the bed, and held it up. Sophia tried to grab it, but failed. Mason helped her to lean over and pulled back her hair while she threw up. She fell back weakly against the pillow, and then immediately tried to sit back up.

"Just lie down," Duffy insisted.

"Can't it's making the room spin." Mason found the remote and brought the bed up into a sitting position.

"Thanks, boyfriend." She gave a wan smile.

"Fiancée. You need to get these things right for when the doc gets back." She took a deep breath in through her mouth.

"I'm going to go get a fresh pan." Duffy darted out of the cubicle.

"Why are you here?" she asked him.

"I've got to hold the gauze." She arched an eyebrow.

"To tell you the truth I don't really know. I had to come." She looked at him in confusion, like nobody had ever been there for her before. Her next words proved it.

"Seriously, you didn't need to. I'll be fine." She gave a guilty look to his jacket sitting on the chair in a corner. "I'll have that dry-cleaned." Was she out of her mind?

"Honey, it's fine." She reached up and grabbed the gauze.

"I can hold it you don't have to." It was clear she didn't want to be a bother.

"I'm your fiancée. What would the doctor think if I left?" She laughed. "But seriously Sophia, I'm fine to do this tonight."

Duffy came back with a new clean pan. "So do you feel up for questions?"

"Not really, I'd prefer to put this out of my mind? Is there Clorox for bad memories?" her voice sounded so forlorn.

"Ah sweetie, I wish there were." The cop was one of the good guys.

"Okay, let's get this over with." Sophia grimaced.

Mason was impressed how the officer asked the questions thoroughly yet kindly. He never made Sophia feel demeaned. The only time Sophia broke down was over her worry for her brother and the unknown woman. She was beaten, bruised and cut, and she was thinking of others. She was amazing. It was obvious Duffy thought so as well. As Duffy was closing his notebook the doctor came back.

"Okay, let's take a look at you." He pulled back the gauze. "How'd this happen?"

"Would you believe a bar fight?" Sophia asked. The doctor frowned at her. "It's a broken beer bottle. I was attacked."

"Anyplace else you were hurt?" he asked briskly.

"That's the main place," Sophia said.

"Her chest and her ribs. I also saw a guy sitting on her legs," Mason interrupted. Sophia looked at him and her eyes were wide with shock.

"The wedding's off. I didn't know you were a tattletale," she said with mock horror. Mason laughed out loud. He was trying to take her mind off a terrible set of circumstances, but she was giving as good as she got.

The doctor looked from one to the other, clearly not knowing how to take them.

"Do you want him in the room with us while I examine you?" In a second, her brave front crumpled and she looked lost, her green eyes were huge. He wanted to hug her, but there didn't look like a spot on her body that wouldn't hurt. He went with his gut and bent over and kissed her forehead.

"I'm going to leave, honey. I'll be right outside the curtain, and then I'll be back when he puts in the stitches," he assured her.

She nodded and gave him a grateful smile. He couldn't make out what was being said, but he heard the small screech she made at one point.

"We need to get you to X-Ray," he heard the doctor say. Jesus, what had those animals done to her? Mason waited for what seemed like forever before the curtain was pulled back.

"You can come back in. I've just given her something for the pain and something to numb the area and cleaned it out. We need to get her up to X-Ray, but I know they're backed up so it could be a while." Mason moved over to her left side and Sophia held out her hand. He was more than happy to hold it.

"It's pretty ragged, you'll want to consult with a plastic surgeon later on," the doctor said matter-of-factly, as he closed the wound.

"I'm having trouble moving it. Will that be permanent?" Sophia tried to reply in kind, but fell short.

"Nope don't worry, this didn't damage the muscle or nerves," the doctor assured her. Sophia didn't watch as he sewed her up, instead she gave Mason a shaky smile.

"X-Ray is actually ready for her," a nurse said as she pushed passed the curtain.

"We were due a miracle," the doctor muttered.

"How are all the people from the wreck?" Sophia asked.

"It's been bad. We had to airlift some up to Mission Hospital. We had fatalities. It was a drunk driver." She gave Mason's hand a tight squeeze. He hated to hear about those kinds of accidents.

"Nurse, I'm done here. I need pictures of her ribs. I'm hoping they're just bruised, but better safe than sorry." The doctor looked at Mason. "You'll have to stay here. She'll be back in about twenty minutes."

"Mason, you don't need to stay." He looked at the woman with the bruised face, green eyes, and honey blonde hair, and knew he'd be staying even if it was for all night.

"I'll be here," he assured her in a soft tone.

When they finally brought her back the pain was obviously worse and they gave her more medicine, which made her very sleepy.

"Sophia, we're just going to have you rest down here for a bit longer. If we can, we'll get you a bed upstairs. If not, you'll just spend the night downstairs with us, is that okay?"

"Whatever you want." Sophia waved her good arm and gave them a goofy smile. Mason and the nurse laughed.

"So you're not admitting her?" Mason asked.

"We don't have a room right now. We want to keep her overnight for observation. You can take her home tomorrow."

"I can go home by my...my...my shelf." Mason laughed with the nurse again. Sophia looked at them both and then she started laughing too

"I'll be here tomorrow, Sophia. I need to get my truck and get cleaned up." He grinned.

"No need," she slurred.

"I'll be here, I promise," his voice was firm, and he gave her his best commander voice.

"I'm fine," she insisted. The nurse gave him a sideways glance as she and the orderly started to wheel the bed to a corner.

"That's my fiancée, always thinking she can handle things on her own," Mason joked.

"Can. Can take care of myself. Always do." It was the last thing he heard as the bed was pushed into the cubicle and the curtain pulled closed.

*　*　*

Sophia remembered small moments of time from being overnight in in the ER. She definitely remembered the stitches they gave her. Thirty-two in all. There had been so much activity because of a huge pile-up on the freeway, and was why she had slept in the ER.

Actually, it wasn't all she remembered. She remembered Mason. She remembered him being so nice and funny. She was pretty sure it wasn't just the drugs either. Could he be anymore wonderful? First he saved her from being raped, and then he pretended to be her fiancée and kept her company for hours. Come to think of it, it must be the drugs.

One of the few things she did remember clearly was using a phone to call Margie yesterday to say she wouldn't be able to make it into work, because she would be looking for Billy. She felt bad lying, but better that than Margie seeing her this busted up. But now all she had to do was get the hell out of the hospital, figure a way to her car, sneak in the back way to the diner without anyone seeing her, and fall into a dead coma.

The nurse was nice enough to give her two hospital scrub tops, since she didn't have a bra. They also gave her some pre- scriptions for pain medication she hadn't intended to filled. She'd seen how out of it the narcotics made her mother be- fore she died, and she hated the thought of taking them. But now she realized how bad the pain was in her shoulder and everyplace else, she guessed she was going to have to get them filled after all.

She figured the hospital was about eight miles away from her car. It was going to hurt to walk there. Her legs were bruised from when the man had slammed down on top of her to keep her still, but she didn't have a ride, and she knew Margie was busy at the diner and the DeLuca's were busy at the pantry.

One of the nurses told her she would be okay to leave at nine a.m. They had wanted to keep her overnight for obser- vation in case she had a concussion. It was eight thirty in the morning and she was antsy to get the hell out of the hospital. She tied her sneakers one handed, which she saw as quite a success for the day.

The curtain opened with a flourish.

"You really should have waited for a minute I could have helped with that," the nurse said.

Sophia looked up and saw the woman from earlier standing next to a big man who looked familiar. She did a triple take. Mason was shaved and shiny and wearing a button down shirt instead of a T-Shirt. The man wasn't a pretty boy. He was rugged. His hair was sun-streaked brown, he was tan from the California sun, and he had the most kissable lips. Dammit those drugs must be more powerful than she thought. Keep it in your pants, Anderson.

"I brought your ride," the nurse said. "I'm going to get your wheelchair. I'll be back in a jiffy."

"You're my ride?" Sophia asked wide-eyed.

"Yes, your ride home," he said. "Remember last night you asked me to take you home?" Sophia kept staring at Mason, but now she saw the length and breadth of him, and that looked familiar too.

"Do you surf?" She ran her good hand through her hair while she wondered if she was losing her mind.

"What?"

"Do you surf Moonlight Beach?" she repeated the question slowly.

He rubbed the back of his neck and gave her a hard stare. "Yeah, I do. How do you know that?"

"Engaged people should know things about one another." She felt a sense of satisfaction that he was now off guard. He continued to stare at her and finally smiled. Damn, he had a great smile. What the hell was he doing there? He had done enough. And how in the hell had it turned out that the surfer she ogled for five days straight ended up being her rescuer?

"How did you know to come here?" Lines showed between her eyebrows.

"He called of course," the nurse said as she wheeled in the chair. "I told him you were being discharged at nine o'clock. He told me you would be trying to leave earlier." Damn, how had he known?

"Let's get you into this chair." The nurse pushed down the footrests.

"I don't need that." She could make her way on her own two feet even if it was going to hurt.

"Hospital rules." There were always rules, Sophia figured. She sat in the chair and started to slip her arm out of her sling so she could wheel herself.

"Honey, I'm going to push you. Put your arm back in the sling," Mason said in a gentle command.

"So what's my new last name going to be again?" She looked over her shoulder at him.

"Gault." He chuckled. "Let's get you out to my truck and you can tell me where to take you."

He parked her at the front doors of the hospital and then jogged to his vehicle. She was not surprised when he drove up in a large black truck that looked like she would need a crane to get in. He opened the passenger door and came back for her.

"I can walk now," she said hoping he wouldn't push her in the wheelchair anymore.

"I'm sure you can," he said as he picked her up. She let out a small screech.

"What the hell?" she asked in a loud whisper not wanting to cause a scene.

"You're in pain, aren't you?" he whispered back.

"Well d'huh." Her attempt at humor came out as a groan.

"So let's minimize it where possible. It doesn't hurt me to carry you and it hurts you to walk. It's an easy fix." He had her buckled into the passenger seat before he finished with his argument.

"Now, where do I take you?" He sounded all business like.

"To Encanto Park."

"You want to go on a picnic?" He was smiling kind of. But he didn't start the car, instead he stared at her.

"That's where I left my car." She cut her eyes over at him.

"What did the doctor say about driving with your arm like that, Sophia?" The warm tone didn't fool her, he was going to be bossy about the whole thing.

"He said I shouldn't but I don't have a choice. So please take me to park."

"You do have a choice. I can take you home." *Yep, bossy.*

"And how do you propose I get my car to my apartment?" she asked in as reasonable a tone as she could muster. Who in the hell was he to butt his head into her business?

"I'll drive it to your place. Later one of my teammates and I will get you your car. It's easy. Now where do you live?" How could he sound so reasonable when he was being so unreasonable?

A horn honked as someone from behind them got impatient.

"We need to go, they're waiting." Sophia gestured to the car behind them.

"We're not going until this is settled. Honey, where do you live?" His sky blue eyes stared at her intently and she realized he would remain in the passenger pick up lane until she answered him. She tried one last time.

"I'd really prefer it if you would take me to the park." This time her voice came out almost pleading.

"Sophia, it's not safe. I'm not sure it's even legal. Haven't they given you something in the hospital for pain? Should you be behind the wheel of a car?" Damn it, he was right, but she really didn't appreciate his high-handed manner. What's more, she didn't like people to know where she lived. Not that she was ashamed of it, but it was safer to remain anonymous. She sat there. The horn honked again, but he didn't move and he didn't take his eyes off hers. He didn't seem impatient, as a matter of fact, he only looked caring. She finally told him to head to San Clemente.

When they pulled up to the diner, Mason grinned.

"You wanted breakfast first? This is a great idea, I'm starved." He kept driving down another two blocks until he saw a parking spot. "Let me circle back and drop you off so you don't have to walk and then I'll park. I can take you to breakfast and we can get to know one another." Sophia didn't have the heart to tell him this was where she lived since it was obvious the man needed to eat breakfast.

"Okay, I'll wait for you inside." She knew this was not going to go well when she made an appearance and she was right.

"Sophia! My God girl, what happened to you?" Margie came over and just stood and stared. Before she had a chance to answer Margie started to cry.

"Hey, it's okay. It's not as bad as it looks." Sophia awkwardly stroked the older woman's forearm with her left hand.

"What happened?" Sophia slipped her arm out of her sling and put her arms around the older woman and then groaned in pain.

"Sophia, put your arm back in the sling," she heard Mason say. Sophia and Margie both lifted their heads to look up at the formidable man standing in the diner doorway.

"It's fine," Sophia lied as she cautiously eased it back into the sling.

"Your poor face. Sophia, what happened to you? Baby, let me get you some ice." Margie left Mason and Sophia standing by the hostess stand as she went to the back to get some. Sophia eyed a booth in the back corner, and picked up a menu and motioned Mason to follow her.

"Do you work here?" Mason asked as she slid him the menu.

"Yep. I live above the diner."

"Oh honey, did you just mean to come here and go to bed? Why don't you go and rest. Give me your car keys and tell me the make and model. Drake and I will go and get it and drop it off later." The concern and guilt was evident in his voice.

"No, it's okay. I should eat something to go with the medicine." Sophia tried to make him feel better.

"What medicine?" Margie asked as she brought over an ice pack for Sophia. "Did they give you some pain medicine? Are you actually taking it? You better be Sophia Anderson. You'll just get worse if you can't rest." Sophia looked down at the placemat on the table trying to avoid the two people staring at her.

"You are going to take the medicine they prescribed, aren't you?" Mason asked. His voice sounded like velvet wrapped around steel. Sophia was beginning to respond to it even when he was being bossy.

"If it becomes necessary," she hedged.

"Damn it Sophia, I know you hate medicine but it's necessary. If Billy was hurt you'd make him take it, wouldn't you?" She looked up and met Margie's eyes. She nodded.

"Okay then. Can I bring you the usual?" Margie held her pen high over her order pad and stared down at her.

"Yes ma'am," Sophia said smiling up at Margie. She really loved it that the woman was trying to take care of her.

"What about you boy, what would you like to eat?" Sophia held back a grin at the idea of the man who stood well over six feet being called a boy.

"What's good?" he asked with an easy grin.

"Everything I serve is good," Margie responded proudly.

"Then I'll leave it up to you," Mason said putting a smile on Margie's face.

"Oh, he's a keeper Sophia." Margie winked at her.

CHAPTER FIVE

Mason loved good diner food and this was *excellent* diner food. He was stunned he hadn't heard about the place, because SEALs knew where to go for good chow. The only thing that marred the meal was seeing Sophia in so much pain. Not that she would admit it. It was obvious she was right handed, because she was having trouble eating with her left hand. Then moving her jaw was painful, and Margie had given her Eggs Benedict. Finally she just ate the little bit of egg and hollandaise sauce giving up on the ham and English muffin. He'd gotten mashed potatoes to go with his steak and eggs. He forked them all on to her plate. She gave him a shy smile.

"So will it be okay if we bring your car tomorrow instead of today?" Mason asked casually.

"Oh no, I need it today." *Gotcha.*

"Are you planning on making another trip down to the Encanto tonight?" Mason asked in an offhanded manner as he forked in another piece of steak.

"Uhm, no. I mean I can't not with this sling and all." Even with the bruises on her face her blush was obvious. The woman couldn't lie to save her life.

"Then why do you need your car?" he demanded.

"I don't. I just didn't want to leave it down there longer than necessary. It's not a safe place." Sophia continued to fumble her way through the lie.

"No shit." Mason continued to eat. It was one of the things he'd learned, no matter what the situation you had to fuel your body. "So you want to rescue your car and not your little brother, huh?" She continued to take small bites of the potatoes. Apparently she was only going to fall for his offhanded questions one time.

"I can help you look for him." There was no way she was going out there alone.

"Mason, I don't know you. You have your own life. I'm not going ask you to help." Damn he admired her, even if she was fighting a losing battle.

"You haven't. I'm offering." That made her look up. Apparently she wasn't used to people offering help. Her chin jutted out.

"He's my brother. He's my responsibility."

"According to the cop last night he's in foster care so he's the state's responsibility." Now the chin came up.

"He's my brother. My *baby* brother. My mother got sick and couldn't take care of him and he ended up in foster care. As soon as I can, I'm going to petition for him to come and live with me." She pointed her fork at him for emphasis.

There was a lot that wasn't said in those few sentences. Where was her mother now? Where was her father? Why couldn't she petition to take him in now? Why in the hell did he care so much? Time for another tack.

"How did you know I surfed at Moonlight Beach?" His eyes narrowed as he watched her take another tiny bite.

"I would eat breakfast there some mornings." His mind went back in time. It was right after South America. He'd been trying to get his head together after losing men under his command. Then it hit him.

"You had a pink blanket and a red sweater." Again she blushed.

"Do you surf?"

"No but Billy did before Mom got sick and Dad left." She had to be kidding. Her dad left after her mom got sick? What a bastard.

"Let's not beat around the bush, okay?" She stared at him.

"Wouldn't it be nice to have help finding your brother?" He waited, and she finally gave him a small nod. "I'm really good at finding things when I put my mind to it."

"Look, Billy will be scared when he hears some guy is out looking for him. It's better if it's me." At least she was really giving his comments consideration, even if she was trying to dismiss them.

"Fine, we'll look together." Mason didn't like that option. He would have preferred she stayed there and rested, but chances were she'd just go out and look on her own. Plus, she was probably right, the boy would be more likely to come out of hiding if he knew it was his sister searching for him.

"Can we leave now?" she asked hopefully. He looked at the little bit of food she'd eaten and the pallor of her face.

"How about if I come back in four hours so you have a little time to rest? It will also give me some time to talk to some of my friends who know their way around downtown."

"But..." she started to protest.

"Look at your wrist." She looked down and saw that her wrist was now resting in her plate of food. She blushed in embarrassment. "You're so tired you don't know if you're coming or going," he said gently.

"You'll be back in four hours? You promise?" God she was stubborn.

"I promise. I'll be back with your car and with my friend Drake." He used a soothing tone, when he really just wanted to order her to go up to her room and sleep.

"Okay."

"Do I have your word you'll rest?" Shit, he was sounding like a lieutenant.

She tugged at her honey blonde hair and finally nodded. He hoped she was telling the truth.

* * *

"A nineteen nineties baby blue Cadillac? They sure don't make them like this anymore," Drake said as he took his second walk around the car and whistled. It was grating on Mason's nerves.

"Drake, I said I would drive it," Mason threw his keys at Drake's chest. Drake's eyebrows raised.

"What, I'm not allowed to make fun of one of the worst POS's I've seen since high school?"

"No, you're not." Mason got in and saw the duct tape that had been used to hold up the ceiling liner, and repair some of the splits in the upholstery. But then he saw the angel that was affixed to the sun screen and smiled. The interior of the car was spotless. He would bet money this had been Sophia's mother's car.

Drake knocked on the driver's side window. Mason rolled it down. "Yeah?"

"I'm sorry man, I was only having a little fun." Drake was sincere. Mason loved that he *got* it.

"Yeah, I know, but dial it down, okay?" It pissed him off that Drake seemed to be making fun of Sophia.

"Tell me what's up before we get there." Drake gave him the same penetrating look he would before an operation.

"I told you how I found her, and I explained the stint at the hospital, and going to the diner."

"Yep, that's my lieutenant, riding to the rescue. So tell me everything you didn't tell me before," Drake asked in his second-in-command voice.

"She's balancing on the head of a pin but she's got this huge well of pride. She's been knocked down and somehow she's gotten up and she leads with her chin. Fuck man, she's amazing. This car is just another part of her. Here she is in the worst part of town and driving this piece of shit. Still she's bound and determined to find her brother when the cops and social services can't." Mason shook his head. He couldn't believe her gumption, and it sent a shiver of fear up his spine. What would have happened if he didn't have insomnia and hadn't been there to help her?

"Got it." Drake gave him a solemn nod.

When they got to the diner it was the middle of lunch hour, but there was a table with a reserved sign on it. Apparently it was not the norm by the grumbling of the patrons in line waiting to be seated. Sophia was taking orders so she missed them when they came in, but when she turned around she smiled.

"She's beautiful, Mase." She was. She also shouldn't be working. Even from there, Mason could see the lines of pain around her mouth. He looked around for Margie and caught her eye. Margie bustled over to him.

"I'm so glad you're here. She came down about an hour ago and put the reserved sign on the table for y'all. I couldn't stop her from working until you showed up. Even though Brenda and I have things mostly covered. Now that you're here, please sit down for lunch." Margie patted Mason's arm.

"Hello," Sophia stopped in front of him. She smiled at Drake.

"Sophia, this is my friend Drake Avery who I was telling you about. Drake, this is Sophia Anderson. Sophia, come sit down and eat with us." Mason smiled at Sophia, taking in the bruising on her face.

"After you explain why you're working. Are you out of your mind, girl?" Drake demanded. Oh, this was not going to go well. Of course it was exactly what he was thinking, but he would have said it with a little more tact.

"This way to your seat." She turned and ushered them to the table with the reserved sign. Mason held out a chair for her but she ignored it and walked towards the back of the diner. Yep, tact would have worked better.

"What the hell?" Drake said loudly.

"Shut it," Mason hissed. He followed Sophia towards the kitchen. He thought she might be going back there to work, and then saw a small door to the right that had to be to the upstairs apartment. She fumbled with the doorknob with her left hand and he took the opportunity to put a gentle hand on her uninjured shoulder.

"Honey, can we talk?" He tried to catch her eye, but she kept looking at the doorknob.

"I'm going to wait upstairs until you're done with lunch." Dammit, she probably hadn't even eaten lunch. He was going to kill Drake.

"I missed you, and I sure would like it if you'd have lunch with me." She paused and turned to him, her green eyes unsure.

"You did? Me?"

"Yes, you. I would really like to spend more time with you. If you don't eat with me, I'm stuck eating with just Drake. Would you really force me to endure that?" Her eyes twinkled at his teasing.

"He can be a little overbearing, can't he?" Seeing her smile hit him in the gut. He'd love it if she'd do it more often.

"He's a SEAL—it's in the job description."

"Holy crap. Are you one too?" Her eyes widened.

"If I answer this wrong, will you still have lunch with me?" She hesitated. Damn, most women were all over him when he said SEAL. "Sophia?"

"I don't want to take up too much of your time. You must be busy and I can look for Billy by myself." Yep, being a SEAL was counting against him.

"Let's go have lunch and put Drake in his place. Then we can talk about my schedule and how best to find Billy, okay?" He waited and she finally nodded. Okay, he'd managed to get past another hurdle and he breathed a sigh of relief.

* * *

She was having lunch with two Navy SEALs. The last twenty-four hours couldn't be more surreal. Maybe it was a waking dream. She'd hardly slept since they'd told her Billy ran away. She'd slept for a few hours in the hospital thanks to the miracle of painkillers, but the bad dreams soon had her sitting straight up. She had hoped being back in her own bed would make a difference, but all she kept picturing were the two men cornering her, stripping her, and touching her.

She shook her head slowly, but nothing changed, she was still at the Omega Grill with two of the most mesmerizing men she'd ever seen.

"What are you shaking your head about, honey? Don't you like your food?" Mason leaned forward to catch her gaze.

Sophia looked at the shredded chicken smothered in gravy with the soft dumplings. Margie had damn near put her meal through the blender. Still, it tasted divine, but there was too much. She looked at the other two meals on the table and realized that Margie had been just as thoughtful. The guys had gotten meals on steroids. They'd only been seated for five minutes and they were both halfway done with their huge plates.

"Sophia?" Mason prompted.

"I'm sorry, what did you say?" She needed to get her head in the game. Mason Gault was too sexy for his own good, and Drake Avery wasn't far behind. Both of them were making it hard to concentrate.

"I asked if you liked your food." He looked like he was trying to figure her out. She didn't need him trying to piece her together like a puzzle.

"Oh, it's fine. There's just too much." She gave the best smile she could muster.

"Whatever you don't eat pass my way." Drake grinned. "This place is killer. Why haven't we ever heard about this place, Mase?"

"Beats me. Honey, you need to eat more than that." Sophia looked down and realized she had probably only eaten five or six bites. He was right, if they were going to be checking out the streets of downtown San Diego all night, she'd need to eat more. She took another bite, letting the flavor melt on her tongue.

"So are you from around here?" Drake asked.

"I was born in Manhattan Beach. We kept moving more and more south over the years," Sophia answered. "How about you?"

"I was born in Tennessee. I'm the oldest of seven kids. The only way to get a college education was the military and I wanted a degree in engineering." If she hadn't been so tired, she would have noticed his southern accent before now. She turned to Mason.

"I'm from Portland, Oregon. My dad was in the Navy and I always planned to be a SEAL." He was clearly proud of his father.

"You put him anywhere close to water and you'd think he was Aquaman." Drake laughed. "He loves the water."

"Isn't that a job requirement?" Sophia asked.

"SEAL stands for Sea, Air, Land. You've got to love it all. I'm a better flyer than Mase, but that doesn't mean I love it. I'd say I love the land part of it the best. But Mason, he loves the sea."

"I've seen him surf," Sophia blurted out. Then she wished the words would go right back into her mouth again. Drake lifted his eyebrow.

"You have? Tell me more," Drake drawled.

"Cut it out. Let's just have a nice lunch. Let's not ruin it. Sophia, aren't you going to eat anymore? How about just a little?" Mason coaxed.

"Come on Sophia, you haven't eaten enough to keep a bird alive," Drake said.

"What?" she exclaimed.

"Damn, that came out wrong. It's just easy to worry about you." Sophia cocked her head and looked at Drake.

"Why would you be worried?" Now she was confused. The two men stared at one another, and then Mason covered her left hand where it was resting on the table.

"Sophia, can you look at me for a moment?" She turned to him. "You're trying to do too much. You've just been badly beaten. You're in pain and you probably can't sleep."

Sophia waited a moment, enjoying the heat of Mason's hand, before she pulled hers out from underneath his. She turned away from him and looked into the intense gray eyes of Drake Avery.

"Ma'am, I'm sorry I came on so strong. Mase told me about you, and I could see he was right, you need a keeper." He smiled warmly as he inadvertently ground her feelings into dust.

"Jesus, Drake. Shut the fuck up," Mason ground out. "Sophia, I never, ever said you needed a keeper. What I said was I was worried about you and I wanted to help you. This is Drake trying to help. This is why he'll always be single."

Sophia had been pushing out her chair to leave the table when Mason made the last statement. She stopped and stared at him.

"Guess I kind of overshot my landing with that one, huh?" The man was making zero sense, but she couldn't feel her legs so she couldn't very well leave. "I was really hoping to ask you on a date, and I think I better do it now before Drake ruins any chance I might have with you."

She couldn't have stood up if her life depended on it. Was the man insane? Even before her face was black and blue she was hardly ever asked out, and certainly not by men who looked like Mason Gault. There was obviously some kind of mistake or some kind of game going on. She looked between the two men. Were they having fun at her expense? Her eyes started to water and this time she was able to get up.

She heard him calling her name as he followed her, but she refused to look back. She needed to get up to her apartment while she still could manage it. Her one eye was puffy, and now that the tears had started she was really having trouble seeing. She grabbed at the doorknob, but it wouldn't turn. Dammit, her palm was sweaty. She wiped it off on her jeans, and tried again. Still wouldn't turn. Please God, don't let her cry. The damn doorknob just wouldn't turn.

"Let me." She had no choice but to let Mason open the door. As soon as it was open she pushed passed him and shot up the stairs. Then she was confronted with another doorknob and he was there again. She waited and let him open the door and again pushed passed him into the small room that was her apartment. It was one big room, the only separation was for the tiny bathroom. Three steps and she was in the middle of the place. She turned around and saw him standing at the doorway with a concerned expression.

"Will you tell me what's wrong?" Mason held his palms outwards as if to get her to stop moving.

"What's your game? I don't understand your game, Mason. It's making me crazy." She watched as concern turned to hurt.

"This isn't a ploy." He looked her dead in the eye and she shivered.

"Look at me, no one wants me, I'm nothing like the girls around here. I'm skinny and plain." She lifted the arm in her sling so he could see everything. She was proud she kept the tremble out of her voice. "I really appreciate you bringing me my car, and the ride from the hospital, but you don't have to do anything more for me."

"I *want* to help you." He walked into the room and lifted his hand and cupped her cheek.

"If you want to help why are you making fun of me?" She still was talking without coming apart, so it was good.

"How am I making fun of you? You need to explain what you're talking about. I'm in the dark here."

"You can't really want to go out on a date with me. Look at you. Guys like you don't date girls like me." His eyes darkened, and his thumb stopped moving on her cheek. He took a deep breath, then another, and then a third.

"In the last four days, how many hours of sleep have you had?" He'd gone so still. Was he mad? He seemed mad.

"Answer the question," he commanded.

She flinched at his tone. "Are you mad?" she voiced the question she had been thinking.

"Honey, can you answer my question?" His thumb stroked her cheekbone again. It felt so good.

"Maybe ten or twelve hours in the last four days." His other hand came up, and cupped her other cheek, his touch so gentle. How could blue eyes be so soft, so warm, so inviting? He brushed a soft kiss across her lips. She kept her eyes open, staring into his. Little lines fanned out at the corners of his, and he smiled.

"Honey, I think you're adorable, and I really, really do want to go out on a date with you. Do you want to know something else that's true?" She nodded.

"I'm scared to death if we go downstairs Drake will say another dumb shit thing and you'll run away again." She smiled, knowing he was probably right. "You have to promise me when we've found your brother you'll go out with me, no matter what Drake says or does."

"But..." He cut her off before she could say no.

"Sophia, I'm only allowing you the one time mistake of putting yourself down because you're obviously sleep deprived. Honey, the reason I call you that is because you're so sweet. I have never called another woman honey." God, she wanted to believe him. Then she had a flashback to her dad and pulled away from him.

"That sounds really good but I don't believe you," her voice trembled though she wanted it to sound firm.

"Again, I'm going to put this down to sleep deprivation. In the meantime, you have two SEALs at your disposal. We're not leaving. So you might as well make use of us." His determination was obvious, and she really needed help to find Billy. He had been missing for five nights. She couldn't stand the thought of her brother out there alone for a sixth.

"Thank you." She smiled up through her lashes.

"You're welcome 'honey'." She wished she didn't like it so much when he called her that.

CHAPTER SIX

As they got into the truck, Mason tried to get Sophia to take the front seat, but she wouldn't, insisting Drake needed the leg room.

"She's right man, I do." Mason scowled at his friend.

"Can we stop at the phone store?" The question was asked so quietly he almost missed it as he started the engine.

"Damn Sophia, I should have thought of that. I had to go yesterday since mine was lost. Yours was damaged wasn't it?" He looked over his shoulder and saw her nod.

"I wouldn't ask, but I left Billy's picture with the missions and shelters, and they said they would call me if he showed up." She was holding her broken phone in her hand as if she were willing it to ring.

"Sure, let's go."

After they got her a new phone they headed into the city. Mason was familiar with many parts of San Diego since he'd bought an old house in Lincoln Park and started renovating. His dad had done construction, so doing the work on his home in San Diego made him feel close to his dad. His house was in an older part of town that was full of good hard-working people. He would work late into the night restoring the floors or the woodwork, and then go for long walks to work out the kinks. He hated to admit he'd also had trouble sleeping, so he understood where Sophia was coming from.

It never bothered him walking through Encanto even though it was considered one the worst parts of San Diego. He often brought a couple of extra sandwiches to give to some of the homeless. That's what he'd had been doing when he came upon Sophia. It still scared the hell out of him to think what would have happened if he hadn't been there.

"Billy stayed at the Union Mission last night," Sophia said as he parked his truck in the park's parking lot. "I just got a text."

"That's great, I know where that is." He started the engine and headed towards the mission. Drake had been abnormally quiet the closer they had gotten to the park. Mason was worried what was coming, and as they pulled up to Union Mission, Drake let loose.

"Where in the hell are we? This can't be part of San Diego. Jesus, Sophia, you're not allowed to be out here during daylight hours let alone at night," he roared.

Mason looked up at the sky praying for help.

"Do you have sisters, Drake?" Sophia asked.

"Yes, I have three of them," he automatically snapped out an answer.

"And you're still living? I'm shocked." Mason roared with laughter. Help had come. He knew Sophia had a backbone when protecting others but he'd worried she would never stand up for herself. Apparently his prayers had been heard.

"Are you calling me overbearing, little girl?" Drake drawled.

"I've been calling you many things in my head, Drake, overbearing is probably the only one that is fit for public consumption." Both men laughed.

"But seriously, this is not safe, you can't be out there. You're lucky you're alive." Drake seemed to be on the fence, his expression half dictatorial, and half wheedling.

"Drake, my brother is only twelve years old. He's been out there for five nights. The police haven't found him, what other choice did I have?" Her green eyes filled with tears. Drake looked at Mason, clearly at a loss.

"We'll find him for you, honey." Mason stepped in.

"Don't you have to be at work?" she asked pulling at her hair.

"We go in for training tomorrow morning, but we just got done with an operation so right now we're not active. We have time to help." Hell, Mason would just ask for leave until Billy was found, there wasn't a chance in hell he would risk Sophia's life letting her search for her brother alone again.

When they got inside the mission, Sophia made her way over to the desk at the back. There was an older man sitting at it who immediately got up to greet them.

"Sophia, I'm glad you warned me about your injuries over the phone or I would have had a heart attack. I told you to stop coming to this neighborhood at night," he chided her. He took her left hand into both of his and held it.

"Reverend, I have to find Billy," she said as she leaned into the old man.

"Well you're in luck, I told him I would call you and you would be here for dinner. He promised to be back."

"I don't understand, if he wasn't avoiding you to begin with, why didn't he just call you?" Drake asked.

The preacher and Sophia looked at one another. Sophia finally looked at the two men. "Billy knows I can't keep him right now, so he keeps running away to find our father. Dad lives down here in San Diego, that's how he ended up in San Diego Foster Care instead of Orange County."

"Where is your father?" Drake demanded.

"An old neighbor of ours said he thought he saw dad in Mission Hills. Billy's foster parents are in Rancho San Diego.

I'm amazed he makes it as far west as he does," Sophia said, as the preacher put his arm carefully around her shoulders.

"Why isn't your father in the picture?" Drake wanted to know.

"He took off when my mom got so sick. They weren't happy for a long time and the cancer gave him an excuse to bail."

"What a fuckwad," Drake said.

"Please watch your language," the Reverend admonished. "Sophia, introduce me to your two friends."

"Drake Avery and Mason Gault, please meet Reverend Langley." She smiled fondly at the reverend and Mason.

"Let's get you a seat before you fall down, girl."

"I'm fine. What can I do to help before dinner?" The reverend looked at Mason and rolled his eyes, and Mason chuckled. Apparently he wasn't the only one who ran into her stubbornness.

"You can sit down and take care of yourself. You brought me two recruits who I will put to work, you've done enough." And with that said, the reverend took him and Drake to the kitchen and put them to work with two little ladies making dinner for over a hundred people.

"Hey buddy, I'm going to step out for a few. Can I have the keys to your truck?" Mason knew exactly what Drake was up to and threw him the keys. He kept peeling carrots and talking to Mrs. Wilson.

An hour later Drake was back with his arms full of groceries. "Is there more in the bed of the truck?" Mason asked.

"Yep," Drake said sheepishly.

"Oh, this is wonderful," Mrs. Wilson and Mrs. Cavendish said as they started unpacking the bags.

Mason stopped on his way to the truck when he saw Sophia sitting cross-legged on the floor with four children around her and a toddler sitting on her lap as she read them a story. She didn't see him, and he listened in. It was about a princess of course, and how she couldn't sleep because her bed was uncomfortable—something about a pea under her mattress. Mason was as enthralled as the children with the way she told the story using different voices.

"Dude, what's the..." Drake tried to interrupt.

"Shhh."

"We've got to get..." Mason handed the keys back to Drake and motioned him away.

"You've got it bad." Mason nodded and made the motioning movement again. He didn't move until she said 'the end'. She saw him, and immediately blushed.

"How long have you been there?" Sophia asked as she bit her lip.

"Just for a moment," Mason replied easily. "I thought you were going to take it easy."

"How much easier could I take it than reading stories to children?" The little boy pushed out of Sophia's arms, causing her to gasp in pain. Mason was over by her side in two strides. He wrapped an arm around her ribs and lifted her off the floor. She gasped again. Damn it, he'd forgotten her ribs been injured as well.

"You need to be careful," he admonished.

"It's really nothing." She gave him a bright false smile.

"I've had knife injuries before and it hurt worse than when I was shot."

"You were shot?" Her eyes got wide. "Are you okay? When did you get shot? Should you be sitting down?" He looked at her in disbelief. She was one hundred percent serious. Nobody but his mom ever showed so much concern for him. At least genuine concern.

"Settle, honey. I'm fine, it was a couple of years ago." He maneuvered her to the threadbare couch, nodding to Drake as he brought in yet another load of groceries. Drake gave him a knowing smirk.

"What about the knife wound? Did it heal okay? When was that?" Mason sat next to her left side so he could sit close without hurting her. He looked down and saw her soft blue denim clad thigh next to his and groaned inwardly.

"What did you ask?" How could he possibly be expected to remember her question when he was sitting so close to her gentle curves?

"Are you healed?" she asked again.

"You do realize what I do for a living, right? We go into dangerous situations. Hell, I get injured during normal training." He chuckled. "Imagine doing a little hand-to-hand against Drake."

She looked at Drake as he made his way back to the truck. Damn, how much food had the man purchased, Mason wondered.

"He's huge. I hadn't thought about you guys scrimmaging."

"You're adorable. We call it training." She blushed, and he wished she didn't have any bruises marring her creamy complexion. Every time Mason pictured her delicate face being hit by fists he saw red. He needed to call the police officer and see what the status of the charges were against the animals who hurt her.

"Are you okay? Why are you looking angry?"

"I was thinking about the bastards who laid hands on you. After we pick up Billy, let's go by the police department and see what the status is on your case."

"I'd rather we didn't." She played with the hem of her blouse.

"Okay." He'd stop by himself.

"You're not going to ask me why?" she asked in surprise.

"If you don't want to it's good enough for me."

She looked at him and smiled. "Thank you Mason." He brushed her beautiful honey gold hair out of her face and gently caressed her cheek. A movement caught his attention and he turned. He was looking at another set of green eyes that mirrored Sophia's, and they were staring back at him filled with distrust.

"I think your brother is here." She jerked around and once again gasped in pain. "Slowly, girl." He helped her off the couch, and she rushed over to her brother.

The boy looked like hell. Sophia opened her arms and reached for him, but Billy sidestepped and she gave an audible gasp of emotional pain.

"Billy, why can't I hug you?" she cried.

"I'm dirty," he said, his eyes filling with tears.

"Oh sweetheart, that's nonsense." She pulled him into her arms, and he squeezed her tightly. She didn't say a word, just squeezed him back.

Mason knew even if the hug was rubbing bone on bone Sophia wouldn't protest so he stepped in. He tapped Billy on the shoulder.

"Go easy on her Billy, she's hurt."

Billy stepped back and looked at his big sister.

"What happened to you?" Billy demanded.

"It's nothing really, just some bumps and bruises." She smiled at her brother, and then quickly looked over his shoulder and glared at Mason. Billy caught on and turned to look at Mason, then looked back at Sophia.

"No you're not fine. Did he do that to you?" He asked motioning to Mason.

"Of course not. He saved me." Sophia pulled Mason to her side. "This is Mason Gault and he saved me from the men who attacked me. Mason, this is my brother, Billy Anderson."

Mason held out his hand and finally the boy took it. "Thank you for taking care of my sister. She's really special."

"She really is. It's nice to meet you, Billy."

"Billy, you know it could have been you that got hurt. You have to stop running away. I was so worried about you," Sophia spoke in calm tones, and it was obvious she was used to acting like the parent.

"I'm fine. I couldn't find Dad. Can I stay with you for a few days before you turn me in again?"

"I'm going to call the Bards and let them know I've found you. Not only are Mr. and Mrs. Bard worried, but so are the twins. They've all been worried sick. I'm sure they'll be okay if you stay with me a night or two before we contact DHCS. But I'll only agree if you tell me where you've been for the last five nights." Yep, Sophia was clearly in parent mode.

"Okay," the boy agreed reluctantly.

"Billy, I'm glad you came back and found your sister." Reverend Langley offered his hand to the boy and Billy took it.

"Thanks for calling Soph, sir." Billy edged closer to Sophia for support.

"I came to tell you we would be serving dinner, but I'm betting Sophia would like to get you home. Am I right?"

"You're right as always, Reverend Langley," Sophia answered with a relieved smile.

"I'll give your regards to everyone," the reverend assured her. "Billy, you listen to your sister. She's a smart woman. Even more important is that she loves you." He let go of Billy's hand and made his way to another group of people.

"Let's go back to the diner." She hugged her brother again and kissed him on the top of the head. Mason was happy to see her brother was careful not to hug her too tight this time.

Drake came to stand next to Mason and whispered, "God, he looks like shit. I hope nothing bad happened to him."

"Me too man, me too," Mason said.

* * *

The diner was closed but Margie was waiting for them. After Sophia got Billy showered and into some clean clothes she had stored in her apartment, she went downstairs to talk to Margie. She was stunned to find Mason sitting in a booth with the older woman. She expected him to have left.

"Where's Drake?"

"He caught a ride home with a friend."

"How is Billy doing?" Margie asked.

"Better than last time," she said with obvious relief.

"Jesus. If this is better, what happened last time?" Sophia bit her lip. She really didn't want to talk about it.

"The cops found him being hassled by a pimp. He was scuffed up. Since it was the cops who found him, they took him back to his foster parents. I only got to spend a couple of hours with him in the hospital."

"Is something bad going on at the foster parent's house?" Mason asked in a dark voice.

"No, the Bards are lovely people. Billy is just so angry and hopeful. He wants to confront our dad. He thinks if dad sees him he'll take him in." Sophia let out a sigh.

"But the son of a bitch won't. He should burn in hell." Sophia eyed Margie and let out a shaky laugh.

"Where are you going to sleep tonight?" Mason asked her. He used the tone of voice that made her shiver.

"In my apartment," she answered wondering why he'd asked.

"Yes, but on what? The floor? I'm assuming you gave Billy your bed, right?" Sophia thought about the one lonely futon upstairs and nodded.

"Oh Sophia, I didn't even think of that. With all of your injuries you can't be sleeping on the floor. I'd invite you over to my son's house but there isn't enough room," Margie's voice was forlorn.

"You both will stay at my house. I have two guest rooms that are finished. You just have to put up with a dining room that is gutted." The man was utterly crazy.

"That's wonderful, Mason," Margie said. "I'll go wake up Billy."

"Wait a minute. Billy just got to sleep. I'm not having you wake him up. I'm not going to go stay at some stranger's house." But Mason didn't feel like a stranger.

"He's not a stranger, he's Mason," Margie said echoing her thoughts. "You can't sleep on the floor. Your shoulder and ribs can't handle it." Margie pushed up from the table and headed upstairs. Sophia didn't stop her because she was still in shock. The man was taking over her life, and she said as much.

"Honey, I don't mean to be taking over your life. This is just a temporary solution. I wouldn't have suggested it except that you can't sleep on the floor with your injuries. You know you can't, don't you?" his voice was coaxing, and his blue eyes warm.

"I probably can't sleep anyway. I'm going to end up with nightmares. I could barely sleep at the hospital. Every time I closed my eyes I kept seeing those two men."

"I understand about nightmares believe me. They'll lessen with time. I'm just so sorry you're having them." She looked into his dark eyes and thanked God again he had been there. She knew her nightmares would have been so much worse if he hadn't been there when she'd needed him.

"I don't understand why you keep jumping in and offering your time. And I surely don't understand why you're offering to let us stay at your house." She was getting exasperated. Worse, she was beginning to hope for more than he was probably offering.

"Don't you?" He reached across the table and took her hand, tangling their fingers together. Sparks shot all the way up her arm, and her eyes met his. Impossibly, his eyes got even warmer. He pressed his lips against hers. She'd never been kissed with such tenderness and it made her heart ache. He slid his mouth back and forth and before she knew it she was following him, and as he parted his lips she parted hers anxious for more of him, his flavor, his taste, his essence. His tongue glided along the sensitive back of her inner lip, and she sighed and pushed up hard against him, attempting to get closer, but he pulled back.

"Did I do something wrong?" Sophia's voice trembled.

"Oh no, you're doing everything right, honey." He pushed back his chair and bent over. He lifted her out of her seat and settled her on his lap. He did it softly and carefully so there was no stress to her injured shoulder or ribs. He tilted her chin and this time he plundered her mouth, and her head spun. His fingers feathered along her bruised cheek soothing it. His tongue stroked along hers teaching her a method of touch that caused her breasts to ache and her thighs to clench. The kiss was wet and carnal and surpassed anything Sophia had ever hoped to feel.

When Mason lifted his head, she mewed a protest. He trailed kisses along her jaw, and up towards her ear. "I hear footsteps on the stairs." She wiggled to get off of his lap.

"Steady, Sophia. It's okay if they see me holding you. They're going to see that a lot," he whispered.

"But we only just met," she whispered back.

"Doesn't matter. Doesn't matter at all." Oh what a smile he had.

CHAPTER SEVEN

"She's staying at your house?"

Mason looked at Darius, Clint and Drake. Mason was supposed to go out for beer, pool, and pizza tonight and just told them why he had to bail. Apparently Drake was gossiping since everyone already knew about Sophia.

"Yes, she's staying at my house and so is her little brother. Everything is on the up and up." He scowled at Drake, who shrugged his shoulders and grinned. Instead of parting their ways as they left the building all three of them followed Mason to his truck. "You need to explain this to me, buddy," Clint said.

"I can explain it to you—she's beautiful," Drake supplied.

"Mason has had plenty of beautiful women, and he's never invited any of them to stay at his house," Clint responded. Mason tried to ignore them as he threw his gear into the bed of his truck. They hung their arms over the side, and he realized he wasn't going to get rid of them without an explanation.

"Sophia is different. Can we leave it at that?" he tried hopefully. Darius shook his head. "Fine, why don't you guys come over tomorrow night and meet her and then you'll understand."

"You want us to meet her? This is just getting weirder and weirder," Clint said.

"No it's not. You really need to meet her, she's something else," Drake enthused. Then he looked over at Mason. "Wait a minute. Is this really for them to meet her, or is this just a way for you to get free labor to work on your dining room?" Drake asked.

"Billy needs some time with good male role models. I was really hoping you might get a chance to talk to him, Darius."

"Is he having a hard time with his foster parents? We need to talk to DHCS. Is he here in San Diego County?" Mason watched as Darius pulled out his cell phone. Darius grew up in the SD foster system, which is specifically why he wanted Billy to meet him. But of course Darius, being Darius, would be ready to make calls and take names if he thought a child was in trouble.

"Whoa there buddy. According to what Sophia has told me, the Bards are good people." Mason knew he'd better rein in his friend.

"Then why does he keep running away?" Darius demanded. Mason rubbed his hand through his hair.

"Look, it's part of why I want you to come over tomorrow. And so you can meet her and I don't have to put up with twenty questions. Seriously Darius, if I thought the foster parents were a problem don't you think I would have stepped in?"

"Well yeah," the man admitted.

"Okay. You guys go have a great time with your beer and pool I'm going home. I'll see you tomorrow." He waved, grateful to have such loyal friends.

Mason headed back to his house. He was thankful Margie managed to talk Sophia into not going to work for the next three days. She was still in a lot of pain. Margie made it seem like it was to spend time with Billy, but it was just as much to let Sophia rest.

As he drove home with the windows rolled down, he once again reveled in the perfect Southern California weather. When he got to his house he smelled something heavenly. *Dammit.*

"Hello," he called out loudly, not wanting to startle either Anderson.

"We're in the kitchen." Like he couldn't figure that out.

There were two pies resting on a rack, and Billy was taking out a baking sheet of chocolate chip cookies from the oven. He was covered in flour and was smiling from ear-to-ear. Maybe Sophia hadn't overdone it, maybe she had Billy do all of the heavy lifting. He turned and saw her big grin as well. His heart melted.

"Mason, you're here just in time to taste test." He went over to the fridge and got out the milk, snagged three glasses and poured them each a glass.

"Do I get to taste test the pies too?" He did a double take, because there was also another pan with a dishtowel over it. "What's this?" He took off the dishtowel and found brownies. He damn well knew he didn't have any brownie mix at home. As a matter of fact he didn't have most of the ingredients needed to make these baked goods.

"Honey, you didn't have to go to this much trouble." He rubbed his ear, wanting to somehow offer her money for the food, but knowing it would offend her and ruin her efforts.

"It wasn't any trouble. Billy and I were remembering how much fun it was when Mom would have a baking day. So we decided to have one of our own." Mason could drown in her sunny smile.

"It was great. We still have to test everything. I don't know if Soph can make stuff as good as Mom." Billy gave his sister a poke in the ribs and Mason saw her flinch.

"Gentle, Billy," Mason cautioned.

"I'm sorry, Soph." He gave his sister a soft hug.

"Billy, we need to talk about how your sister got hurt," Mason said as he cut brownie squares and put them onto plates for everyone. They sat around the kitchen island.

"This isn't really any of your concern, Billy and I will handle it." She turned away from him and gave all her focus to her brother.

"Has Sophia explained how she got hurt?" Mason asked the boy who looked so much like his sister. He was reaching for a second brownie and he stopped.

"We were supposed to last night but I ended up going to sleep. It happened when she was looking for me, right?" Billy looked at Mason with growing guilt.

"That's right." Mason watched as tears filled Billy's eyes, and how he wiped them away with the sleeve of his shirt.

"I'm sorry, Soph. You shouldn't have been out there. I didn't ask you to be," the last was said with the defiance of a teenager. Mason figured at twelve that's basically what he was.

"Billy, if Sophia was missing wouldn't you go out and look for her? Especially if something bad almost happened to her last time?" Mason gave the boy a hard look, wanting him to understand the consequence of his actions.

"Mason, this isn't your business. This is between me and Billy." Sophia looked brittle. She looked mad. He was not scoring any points that was for damn sure.

"I would have gone looking for her," he answered quietly. Mason was impressed, he didn't have to admit it and he could have hidden behind his sister.

"You can't do this again. Both of you could end up seriously hurt or dead next time." Mason tried to soften his tone, but it was too vital for the boy to understand how important his words were.

"But you don't understand." The boy clenched his fist and looked him in the eye, and then over at his sister.

"What don't I understand?" he asked, eyeing the boy steadily.

Billy opened his mouth and then shut it. "May I be excused?"

"Yes." They both watched as Billy left the kitchen. Mason didn't have to wait long.

"That wasn't your place." Sophia threw down the napkin she'd been shredding.

"I'm sorry you feel like that but he needed to hear how he endangered you." She glared at him, and he might have felt bad if her face weren't a rainbow bruise.

"Right now I'm trying to get him calmed down and happy enough to stick it out with the Bard household until I can petition the courts to have him come live with me."

"What makes you think he won't pull this same stunt when he's living with you?" Mason bit out.

"What?" It was obvious the thought hadn't entered her mind.

"You did say he was trying to track down your dad. Well wouldn't he still be trying to do it even if he comes to live with you?" She looked past him towards the kitchen entrance. Then she got off her chair and motioned for him to follow her out onto the back porch.

"I tracked down dad and he's living in Mission Hills. He has a new wife and a baby." Sophia threw out the information.

"Did you call DHCS? He's responsible for Billy."

"That's what I told him. He said Billy isn't his son. He said Mom wasn't faithful to him," Sophia's voice trembled then broke. Once again Mason had to endure the sight of this woman with tears in her eyes.

"Ah honey, I'm sorry." He stepped forward and put his arms carefully around her. He rested his cheek against her silky gold hair. "You do know since they were married at the time of Billy's birth he's still liable for support, right?"

"I do. But he said he'd tell Billy his mother was a whore and he wasn't his father. Mason, he said vile and disgusting things. He called Billy names too. He said he was happy he was in foster care." She shuddered against him. It seemed like the world conspired against this woman, and all she ever did was stand up and try again.

"I don't want to put Billy through that. Because he would do it, Mason. He would." He rocked her back and forth. Finally she lifted her head.

"I'm going to talk to him tonight. Enough is enough. This can't happen again. His safety is paramount. I'll handle it." Mason's first instinct was to say he could join the conversation, but he knew it was something best left between the siblings.

"What are you going to say?"

"I'm at least going to tell him our father has a new family and has moved on. Hopefully that will suffice." She squared her shoulders and he admired her for it.

"I hope you're right."

"Let's go inside, I have some chicken breasts marinating for dinner."

"I didn't bring you to my house so you could cook for me."

"I'm not going to cook, Billy is. The sense of normalcy will do him good. It was one of the things we all used to do together before Mom got sick. It makes us happy. I hope you like chicken." She smiled shyly at him. Hell, he'd like a marinated truck tire if she was serving it to him.

"I love chicken." He opened the door to let them both back into the sweet smelling kitchen.

* * *

She'd tried to sleep the night before but she kept waking every few minutes with the feel of the men's hands on her. More than her shoulder and ribs hurt—her breasts hurt. When she'd looked in the mirror she could actually see fingerprints from where she'd been mauled. Since then, she kept herself covered at all times, even putting on and taking off her bra underneath a towel so she didn't have to see herself.

Tonight she had to get some sleep because she'd almost set fire to one of the dishtowels when she hadn't turned off the gas burners. So she shook out two of the pain pills and huddled under the comforter in the guest bedroom. She waited and waited, checking her phone every fifteen minutes to see if time had gone by and she slept, but she hadn't. She kept yawning. How could she be this tired and unable to sleep? Luckily, she snuck a couple of Mason's books into her room. He had a huge library. She pulled the first two in a series taking place during World War II.

She was still reading when she fell asleep thinking she was driving a jeep for General Eisenhower.

"Sophia, honey, it's okay wake up." A gentle hand. A soothing voice.

"Get away from me." She tried to hit the man but her shoulder hurt, and when she tried to scream he clamped his hand over her mouth.

"It's me, Mason. Please Sophia, honey, it's me. You're safe." It was the smell of him that finally got through to her. Her face was tucked against his chest. Now his hand wasn't covering her mouth she took in deep shuddering gasps of air and it smelled of Mason. She was safe. She was safe.

It was like a dam broke. She started to cry for how scared she had been. She was crying for how dizzy and hurt she was and for the poor young girl who was living her life as a prostitute. She cried for Billy whose mother had died and whose dad was disowning him. And lastly she cried for herself and for the two years she spent taking care of a shell of a woman who often didn't recognize her.

And all the time she sobbed he held her. Not once did he tell her to stop.

"Just let it out. I've got you honey. You're such a good girl. You just let it out." She cried harder because he was saying exactly what she needed to hear. But it wasn't really true, he couldn't be for real, and that made her even sadder.

"Not real...not real...not real," she said over and over as he continued his litany of comforting words.

"What's not real, honey?"

She tried to push away, but his hold was unmovable. Why did she want to push away when nothing ever felt better than being held in Mason Gault's arms?

"What's not real?"

"This. Being here with you." This time when she pushed away he let her. She tried to get up but he stopped her.

"What do you need? Do you want a glass of water?"

"Yes please. And some toilet paper."

"I think we might be able to upgrade to Kleenex." He kissed her forehead and slipped off the bed. Oh God, he was wearing boxer briefs. He looked amazing. This was better than anything she ever imagined when she'd seen him surfing. She was still staring at the doorway when he came back in. He looked behind himself.

"Is there something in the hallway? A spider?" She kept staring, drinking him in. After a moment she saw when he caught onto what she was staring at. He gave her a slow sexy smile. God, it felt like her face went up in a cloud of smoke.

"You are adorable when you blush." He sat back down beside her on the bed, and she looked at his lap. She couldn't help it. For God's sake, what woman could help herself? *They were boxer briefs!* Yep, the man was packing. And then, as she continued to stare, his body had a reaction that made her gaze shoot up to his face.

He was grinning at her. *Grinning.*

"Ms. Anderson, I believe I told you I would like to go out on a date with you. You thought I was kidding. Now we have irrefutable proof. I *definitely* want to go out on a date with you." He handed her some Kleenex.

She didn't know whether to be horrified, embarrassed, or turned on.

"I hope you're as turned on as I am," he said as he took the used tissues and placed them on the nightstand.

"Are you out of your mind? I just blew my nose. You can't be turned on." She hit him on the chest.

"Care to take another look?" She kept her eyes squarely on his face. He handed her the glass of water, and she drank half of it while keeping her eyes on his face. He continued to grin.

"Your brother sleeps like the dead." She handed him the glass and giggled.

"Yeah, I know. I remember Mom would sometimes take the lids off of pot pans and crash them like cymbals to wake him up. Some mornings she would let me do it." Sophia smiled at the memory.

He got up and closed the bedroom door and put the water glass on the nightstand.

"That will stain."

"It's not my focus at the moment. I want to kiss you. Nothing more, just a kiss or two. Then we're going to crawl under the covers and you're going to go to sleep in my arms. If you have a nightmare I'm going to fight the bad guys for you." She couldn't help it, she looked downwards again, and this time there was no mistaking his level of arousal.

"Eyes on mine, honey. He does what I tell him to do. I'm telling him I'm just kissing the pretty girl tonight and then she is falling asleep in my arms." He used one finger to push her chin upwards.

"That doesn't seem fair," she protested.

"Well hell, if I do the kissing right, it won't be fair to you either." She giggled again. God, he was sexy. His eyes, his smile, and that body.

"Shouldn't you be wearing your sling?"

"It's uncomfortable. Anyway, they said I would just need it for a few days, and that the stitches and bandage would be enough."

"It hasn't been even two days yet." He picked it up from the chair with her clothes, and he helped her put it back on. "Humor me." He fanned her hair around her shoulders after he settled the strap around her neck. "You have beautiful hair."

"It's just yellow." She stared at his chest. God, they must do a lot of training. He actually had washboard abs.

"Honey, it's honey, with shots of gold and in the sun I can even see red. Your hair is gorgeous. With as many different facets as you have, don't even get me started on your eyes." She smiled and batted her eyelashes. He laughed out loud.

"You minx, so you know about your eyes? Let me talk about your lips."

"How about I talk about your shoulders?" Sophia touched the top of his big shoulder. He felt warm and his muscles jerked under her touch. She stroked downward so she could drift into his chest hair. It felt so good she couldn't help herself. She leaned forward and pushed her nose close and inhaled the scent of Mason.

"Honey, you need to stop it otherwise we're not going to keep this limited to just a few kisses." His voice was shaky. She smiled and inhaled again. One big hand cupped the back of her head and the other slid down to the small of her back. He pushed downwards with his chest, until she was lying on her pillow looking into the glittering blue depths of Mason's eyes.

She realized this was so much more intimate than the diner. There was just the soft glow of the bedside lamp, and they were in a bed, and he was in a pair of boxer briefs.

In a heartbeat he caught on to her hesitation.

"Sophia, are you okay? Let me go put on my sweatpants. I'll be right back." He started to get up.

"No!" She clutched him. "Don't leave me."

"I'm an ass. I should have thought this through more. You've just been through a horrific event. I shouldn't be in bed with you." He stroked back her hair.

"I can't explain it. I was so turned on but then for a second I panicked. It doesn't make any sense." She stroked her hand down his chest. Touching his skin anchored her.

"It makes sense to me. You had an emotional flashback. It's going to happen." He brushed a kiss against her forehead.

"But you're the one who saved me. I trust you. I want you. Your boxer briefs are killing me. How can I even compare you to what happened in the alley?" Her nails dug into his chest.

"It's going to take time. Your mind and emotions still need to heal."

Sophia licked her lips and considered what he said. His eyes darkened as he watched her.

"Do that again," Mason begged huskily.

"What?" Do what again?" Sophia asked confused.

"Lick your lips."

Sophia slowly moistened her lips with her tongue. He bent closer, and she could almost taste the mint of his toothpaste.

"Again."

She did it again, and he moved even closer.

"One more time."

Sophia pushed out her tongue and started to swipe her lower lip, and he caught it between his teeth. She whimpered. He stroked her captured flesh with his tongue, back and forth causing a frenzy of sensation. She tried to push forward, but he held her captive. She tried to pull back but she was his to do with as he willed. He wanted to play, he wanted to torture. Then he pulled her tongue into the moist cavern of his mouth and sucked. Her nipples peaked and her core flooded. She pushed up, and gasped. He somehow knew the difference, and pulled back.

"You need to do things my way Sophia. I don't want you to hurt yourself."

"I'm not hurting myself," she rushed to assure him.

He looked down at her.

"No lies, not even the little ones, okay? You just hurt yourself when you pushed against me, right?"

She thought about it, she hated making a big deal out of small things, so that's why she said she wasn't hurting herself.

"Mason, I just want to be strong for you. I don't want to sound weak and needy." She looked at the bedspread and avoided his gaze.

He was silent for a long time.

"How in the hell could you ever sound weak? Jesus, Sophia, you're so brave you scare the hell out of me. But here's the deal. I need to know I'm not hurting you. I have to be able to trust you'll be honest with me."

She didn't answer.

"Sophia," his voice commanded a response.

"Okay."

"Now lie back."

She lied down on the pillow and stared at him. He stroked her neck at her pulse point and then placed a kiss on it, sucking gently. As he scraped her with his teeth it took everything she had to stay still. He rained kisses up her jaw and soft kisses on her bruise, until once again he was sipping at her lips and their tongues were tangling. This time she couldn't help when her hips pushed up and met the solid warmth of his cock. When he broke off the kiss she rushed to assure him.

"Nothing hurt this time I promise. It all felt so good."

"That's what I want for you. I want you to have joy and pleasure." Staring into his blue eyes, with his sandy hair falling onto his forehead, she could see his sincerity.

"But you don't know me," she protested.

"Don't I? Think about it. I really want you to think about it." He swooped back in, licking and nipping until she opened, not wanting to miss a bit of taste or flavor of Mason. He retreated, and she grabbed his head.

"No," she tried to pull him back.

"Yes, otherwise I won't be able to stop."

"I don't care, I want this. I want you," her voice breathy.

"It's too soon, honey. We still haven't gone on our date." He smiled, smoothing the hair back from her temples.

"This is a date," she protested.

"This is a gift." He stood and pulled back the comforter. Once again she admired his body and found herself squeezing her thighs together...tightly. Maybe after he fell asleep she could find relief on her own.

"I swear to God I know what you're thinking and you need to stop." He slid in beside her and pulled her into his arms. She blushed, he couldn't possibly know. But then she felt his hand pulling up her sleep shirt and sliding under her panties.

"I think you were thinking about this." His hot breath was warm against her temple.

Oh God, oh God, oh God. Two of his fingers captured the bud of her clitoris, and another circled it. She was so wet he was able to slide and glide. His hand moved her hair as he pinched her bud of nerves. He bit her neck, and she let out a soft shriek as rapture coursed through every cell of her body.

"Now sleep." Sophia melted against his hard body and knew there was no way she could ever fall asleep, until she did.

CHAPTER EIGHT

Mason was on his second cup of coffee when Sophia came into the kitchen. She was wearing her sling with her normal outfit of jeans and a long sleeved T-Shirt. Today's was pink flannel and it looked as soft and touchable as she did.

He pulled out a mug and poured her a cup, moving to the fridge to get the milk. "The sugar is over there," he said. She arched her brow. "I saw how you took it at the diner." She took a sip and sighed.

"You make a good cup of coffee." She stared into her mug.

"I kind of live on the stuff."

"Well it's really good." *Damn, this is awkward.*

"I loved sleeping with you last night." His voice was warm.

She continued to stare into her coffee like it contained the answers to the world's problems. She bit her lower lip, and he about groaned aloud.

"Thank you," she finally said. *Yep, awkward.*

"Did you look around the house? Would you like to hear about the renovations I've been doing?"

Her eyes sparkled. "That would be great. I can't believe you did the work yourself. I know Drake said you did, but I never knew people who could do that."

Giving her a tour, he pointed out where he had pulled up the carpets and sanded down the hardwood floors and restained them. He showed her how he restored the ceramic tiles around the base of the fireplace and re-bricked it so it all matched.

"Did you do the crown molding?" She pointed near the top of the wall.

"Part of it was damaged so I had to match that as well." He guided her hand so it was pointing to an area over a window.

"It all looks the same. That's amazing."

"I'm not nearly as good at this as my father. He's the one who really has a talent for restoring old houses. When I was thinking of purchasing this place, he came down from Portland and looked it over with me." He saw her wistful expression and wrapped a gentle arm around her.

"I think this brings me closer to my dad the same way baking brought you closer to your mom." She nodded her head.

"So when are you going to call DHCS?" Mason kept his tone neutral.

"I called the Bard's the night we found Billy. I knew they'd be worried. I really like them. So does Billy, actually." He waited.

"They told me there's a big test he needs to study for so I need to get him back home tomorrow. I'll tell Billy today that we have to call DHCS."

"I was thinking maybe he'd like to go surfing with me tomorrow morning."

"Really?" She jerked with excitement and her coffee sloshed over the rim of the cup. "Oh my God, let me get a paper towel." She rushed to the kitchen and came back with a towel and wiped up the spill.

"So what are the chances of getting Billy up at the butt crack of dawn?" Mason asked.

"Oh. Yeah, well there's no point. His wetsuit doesn't fit anymore. He's outgrown it." Mason followed her back into the kitchen as she threw away the soiled paper towel. The wetsuit was going to be a problem. Those didn't come cheap. But...

"Sophia, I'm pretty sure we can go rent one today that way he'll have one for tomorrow morning." Mason gave a mental fist pump at the solution.

"Do you think so? What about Moonlight Beach? Isn't it kind of over his skill level?"

"I'll check out the swells. If it's too much we can go surf San Onofre."

"He'd be out of his mind. I can't thank you enough." Her face flushed with excitement.

"Let's get some breakfast. Maybe the smell of bacon will wake him up."

"Oh, you understand how it works, huh?" She laughed.

"I was a growing boy once." Mason chuckled as well.

He was amazed how fast Sophia acclimated to using her left hand. She was chopping the green pepper damn well. When he told her that she smiled.

"I work in a diner. It's not the first time my right hand's been out of commission because of a cut or something."

Mason started the bacon frying and as anticipated, Billy came into the kitchen.

"Hey," the boy said rubbing the sleep out of his eyes.

"Good morning," Mason said in return. He was still amazed at how much the two Andersons looked alike.

"Cool, can I have French toast too?"

"I think that can be arranged," Mason said. Soon there was a mound of food on the kitchen island and they were eating. When Mason told Billy about his idea of surfing, Billy almost choked on the spicy scrambled eggs. He took a huge swallow of orange juice and then wiped his mouth with his sweat shirt.

"Really? You mean it? God, it would be rad!" Then his face fell. "I don't have a wetsuit."

"It's fine. I'm going to rent one for you at a surf shop Mason knows about."

"That's too much money, Soph," Billy objected. "Mason thanks for thinking of me. Maybe some other time."

"William Robert Anderson, I have more than enough money to cover this. Now if you want to argue about it you can call it an early birthday present." Billy gave his sister an assessing look and then got off his stool and threw his arms gently around her.

"This present rocks, sis."

"Yeah, well, enjoy it while you can. Because tomorrow you're going back to the Bard's. You have a math test you have to study for. Rumor has it this is a big one."

"Leslie likes it when I keep my grades up." Billy grinned.

"She's not the only one. Now go finish your food, you've only had enough for two people so far."

Mason watched Billy finish his second plate of food. He mulled over what he'd just seen. Granted, he was an only child so he didn't have any experience with siblings, but it seemed to him the scene between Billy and Sophia was more like a mother and son than a brother and sister. He was really touched how fast Billy was willing to give up his adventure so as not to put a financial burden on his sister.

"I have to go to the base today but tonight I was going to grill some steaks and invite some of my teammates over. How does that sound?" He watched Sophia carefully. He wanted to make sure she was comfortable with the idea of having so many men invading her space. She seemed fine.

"Cool, are they SEALs too?" Billy asked.

"Yep."

"How often do you guys go out on missions? Do you go overseas? Do you have nicknames? Do you carry a gun all the time? Was the training hard?" The boy couldn't sit still to save his life.

"How can I help with dinner?" Sophia asked, clearly trying to stop the avalanche of questions.

Mason answered Sophia's question first, "I've got everything in the fridge. I'm just going to throw it on the grill. Maybe you can help me with the salad and the baked potatoes." She gave a happy smile.

"How many guys are coming over? What are their names? Are you all the same rank? Did you all go through training together? Have any of you ever been injured?"

"Billy, how about you wait until the team comes over tonight, and then we'll talk to you about what it's like to be a SEAL, okay?" Sophia handed her brother his empty plate and pointed him towards the sink.

"This is going to be great," Billy said as he took his dish to the sink.

* * *

Sophia got a call from the police department about the case against the two men who had assaulted her. Dooley and Krill had bonded out. They still hadn't found the young prostitute so her and Mason's testimony would be needed. She was told to expect a call from the D.A.'s office. At the rate things were going she was never going to get to work again.

She called Margie and let her know Billy would be going home tomorrow and she would be coming home to San Clemente, and could open the diner Wednesday morning.

"That's good. I've got to tell you, Sophia, I kind of got spoiled sleeping in for the last few months."

"I think that's wonderful," Sophia enthused.

"What about you? Have you been spoiled lately?" Sophia felt her cheeks heat.

"We had a great breakfast this morning and it's been wonderful to spend time with Billy," Sophia said.

"That's not what I was asking about. Tell me about Mason. He really has taken a shine to you, and if I'm not mistaken you're smitten as well."

"We've only just met." Part of Sophia really wanted to talk to someone about Mason, but another part just wanted to hoard every little detail to herself.

"That's how it was with me and my Stan—love at first sight. Of course that was outside of gym class." Margie giggled. Sophia laughed too.

"Okay, if you're not going to tell me what's going on with your hunky SEAL, then tell me how you're feeling." Sophia moved her shoulder a little bit and winced. But it wasn't as bad as the day before, which she told her boss.

"That's good, but no carrying trays for you. You're on hostess stand duty." Margie's voice was stern.

"You know Brenda likes to seat people," Sophia protested.

"Brenda is lazy. She'll just have to step it up. Anyway she's always saying she needs more money so she can wait tables. I need you to rest. I don't want to see you doing anything but manning the hostess stand." Sophia smiled at the care Margie was showing her.

"And baking. I can still bake one handed."

"Only half pans. If I see you baking full pans of cinnamon rolls or anything else, you're fired."

Sophia laughed at the empty threat, secure in the knowledge Margie liked and appreciated her too much to fire her.

"Okay I might not fire you but I'll be checking up on you. I don't want you putting undue strain on that shoulder, all right?"

"I promise, Margie." It felt odd having so many people concerned about her. "So I'll see you on Wednesday."

"I can't wait and I expect details."

"Seriously, there aren't any details." And Sophia's cheeks heated again.

"The man wanted to take you for a date, what about that?"

"Supposedly we're going this weekend but I don't think we're a good fit." Maybe if they had met when she was more stable. When she'd been going to college and working her part time job at the cable company but not now.

"You sure don't know how to read men. You talk to me when he makes his move, but something tells me he already has. I'll get my info on Wednesday when I see you in person. You can't hide anything with that fair complexion." On that note Margie said good-bye and Sophia went to go get Billy so they could rent the wetsuit.

* * *

When Mason came home with his friends he found the steaks had been marinating, and the baked potatoes were in the oven. All that needed to be done was finish putting the ingredients together for the salad.

He'd left his friends in the backyard and come into the house to get Billy and Sophia and bring them out for introductions.

Sophia was cutting up vegetables, she'd also made fresh guacamole and enough queso to feed an army, or at least four SEALs and a preteen boy.

"I said I was cooking dinner," he said as he put his hand around her, easing his thumb a slight bit under her shirt. Her skin was so soft. She looked at him with startled green eyes as if his little touch came as a surprise.

"You had to work today and this was easy enough for me to do. Anyway, I left the steaks for you to grill." He didn't want to stop touching her, it was addicting, so he stole pieces of carrots and peppers as she chopped.

"Shouldn't you be with your friends? Or offer them something to drink?"

"If they're thirsty they'll come inside." He moved his hand a little higher so it was totally settled on the naked flesh of her lower tummy. Her hand trembled so he plucked the knife away from her and set it down.

"We don't want a kitchen mishap," he explained. She bit her lip.

"You need to stop touching me and go out with your friends. I need to finish up in here." He pulled his hand away and stroked up her arm and then cupped her cheek.

"I don't want to stop touching you. I thought of nothing but touching you all day, except when I was thinking about kissing you. Then when I thought about kissing you, I thought about making you come," he said in a husky whisper.

She whimpered, and he pressed his lips to hers drawing in the sound, and taking in all of her. She didn't part her lips this time, and he knew she was worried someone would see, so he wooed. Licking and lavishing her with brushes of his tongue until finally she succumbed with a sigh.

He thrust his fingers into the silk of her hair and he tilted her head so he could sink in a little further, reveling in her taste, and loving her response. Sophia might have been slow to react but once she did he was a moth to her flame.

"Hmm, hmm," Drake cleared his throat.

He was careful of her arm and ribs as he pressed against her, loving the feel of her slight curves. He slid his hands out of her hair to her lower back. Then further downwards to her ass.

"Little brother coming this way," Drake's voice was low, but Mason heard it clearly. Sophia didn't and wasn't that a huge compliment. Mason eased his hands to her hips so he could edge them apart, loving how she clung to him.

"Sophia. Honey. Billy's coming." She gave him a sultry smile as her eyes focused, and she looked around him.

"Hey Billy." She smiled shyly at her brother.

"Hey Soph. Are you guys dating?" Billy asked as he scooped up a mountain of queso on a chip.

"Uhhhh."

"Oh, they're dating all right." Drake grinned opening the fridge. "Come on out and meet some of the guys, Billy."

"Great. Did you know Mason's taking me surfing tomorrow morning?"

"Yeah, he told me." Drake handed him a soft drink as he pulled out some Pacifico beers and the steaks. "Hey Mason, since you're busy working on the salad I'm going to start the steaks."

Mason watched as his friend handed off the pan of steaks to Billy and took the beers and soft drink out to the patio. He turned to Sophia and grinned.

"So when are you finally going to admit that we're dating?"

"I'm not sure it would be a good idea," Sophia said slowly.

"Why not?" he asked gently.

"It all seems too soon. I'm just confused by it all. You're a bit overwhelming, Mason. Tomorrow I'm going back to my life. I live above a diner. I'm a waitress. I'm saving every penny I can to get an apartment that will be approved by DHCS for Billy to move in with me. I'm just not a good bet for someone like you. You're bigger than life."

"I think we're really good together."

"Well the…" her voice trailed off, and suddenly she found something fascinating on the floor to look at.

"What?"

"The physical part."

"Are you talking about last night?" She nodded her head. "When I helped you get some sleep?" She nodded again without looking up. He crouched in front of her so he could look into her big emerald eyes. "Honey, it was us making love."

"Oh Mason, I wish it had been." She bit her lip, and he couldn't help himself he reached up with his thumb and rescued it. Then her pretty pink tongue took a swipe of his finger and he was lost.

"Jesus, woman, you do it for me. There has never, and I mean never, been a woman who has gotten to me like you have. We're going on a date. And then another, and then another after that." He would have backed off if she gave him any indication she wasn't interested, but she didn't. Instead she seemed to be under the misapprehension this wasn't going to work and he was going to dispel that belief. "Will you put me out of my misery and agree to go out with me this weekend?"

"Yes," she finally whispered.

"Thank God. You sure know how to make a man sweat." She let out a low chuckle, and brushed a lock of his hair. He couldn't help but arch into her touch.

"I'm about done with the salad. Why don't you go outside with your friends and I'll bring out the food?"

"How about we both bring out the food and I introduce you?"

"Okay."

They made quick work of the salad. Then Mason let her carry the big bowl of chips since it was the lightest thing, and he took the dips, the salad, and the dressings.

"I thought we were going to have to send a search party," Drake yelled as they set the food on the picnic table.

"This is Billy's sister, Sophia Anderson," Mason said. "You already know Drake. These other two are Clint Archer and Darius Stanton." Clint and Darius stood up and shook Sophia's hand, and Clint held it a little longer than Mason would have liked. Mason couldn't blame him, Sophia was something else, but he still gave Clint the evil eye and Clint grinned in return. Mason shook his head as he realized his chain was being yanked.

He turned around and saw Sophia had already high-tailed it back into the kitchen. He followed her.

"Sophia, wait up."

"I just wanted to make sure the potatoes aren't over cooking. I hate mushy baked potatoes." She opened the oven with a jerk and poked them with a fork.

"Clint was just giving me a hard time."

She closed the oven door and moved to the refrigerator and started pulling out already chopped chives, whipped butter, sour cream, grated cheese and bacon bits. His mouth watered looking at all the toppings. Then he saw her tense expression and he forgot about the food.

"Seriously, Clint was being an ass. He knows how much I like you so he was flirting with you to get my goat."

"That doesn't make any sense. What makes sense is he thinks we're not together." Fuck, he was going to murder his friend.

"You don't have many guy friends do you." She shook her head. "That's the way guys tease one another. He really was just trying to get a rise out of me and it worked. I wanted to beat the shit out of him for holding your hand too long. Drake thought it was pretty damn funny too."

"He did?"

"Yep."

She looked at him for assurance and when she read his sincerity she smiled.

"Okay, enough with my insecurities, even I'm sick of them. We're going on a date this weekend and I believe your friends think you like me."

"Hall-e-fucking-lujiah, the woman is catching on."

She let out a big laugh, and didn't that deserve a kiss? Before he could get too carried away she pushed at his chest.

"Now I understand what's going on I want to spend some time with your friends."

Mason followed her outside but realized it probably wasn't as easy as she said. Obviously, somewhere her self-esteem had taken some serious hits, probably starting with her father. If the bastard made so many shitty threats against Billy, abandoned their mother when she was sick with cancer, what the fuck had he said and done to Sophia? Yep, Mason knew he was still climbing an up-hill battle with his girl but she was worth it.

* * *

Now that Clint wasn't flirting Sophia really liked him. The men spent a lot of time teasing him. Apparently his flirting was normal, and he had recently winked at a captain's wife. The wife appreciated the gesture, but the captain had not. As a result Clint's captain decided to delegate all of his report writing to Clint, who found himself stuck to a computer screen almost 24/7.

"Clint, I dare you to tell the captain this joke," Darius said.

"Oh God, not a dare," Clint moaned.

"Why is he groaning?" Sophia whispered to Mason.

"For the most part SEALs don't pass up a dare. Clint is in so much hot water with the captain already that adding to it is just mean on Darius' part." Sophia laughed.

Then she thought about it. "Hey Billy, can you go check on the potatoes?"

"I want to hear the joke," Billy whined.

She turned to Darius. "Is it okay for him to hear it?"

"Yeah, it's PG." He turned to Clint with a broad grin.

An admiral and a captain were talking about making love.

The admiral was saying it was seventy percent pleasure and thirty percent work.

The captain disagreed and said it was ninety percent pleasure and ten percent work.

They asked the chief petty officer to settle their argument.

He said they were both wrong.

"If there was any work involved, you would have delegated it all to me," he said.

Clint groaned and rested his head on the table while everyone else laughed.

"He's not really going to have to tell that joke to the captain is he?" she asked the men at the table.

"He sure is," Drake said. "And if he thinks the amount of paperwork he is doing now is bad he hasn't seen anything yet." Mason, Darius, and Clint nodded.

"I deserve an extra baked potato. I saw all the fixings so it's the least I should get," Clint said as he started loading up his plate. All the other men agreed, and Sophia watched as they piled their plates high. She was glad she'd made as much as she had.

"Sophia this is absolutely delicious," Drake said.

"Wait 'til you see all the deserts she made. I like the apple brown betty the best. It's even better than her cherry pies and brownies." Billy looked around the table, enjoying the opportunity to brag about his big sister.

Three sets of wide eyes landed on her.

"Brownies," Drake said on a moan.

"Cherry pie. I love cherry pie," Clint said with glee.

"My mom makes apple brown betty. I never met anyone else who did," Darius said with surprise.

Sophia knew her face had to be scarlet.

"My sister is the best baker in the world. She learned from our mom," Billy said proudly.

Mason squeezed her hand underneath the table, and she gripped it like a lifeline.

"Let me just go in and warm everything up so the vanilla ice cream will melt on it." That was met by sounds of pleasure. Apparently SEALs were easily pleased.

CHAPTER NINE

It took a lot to get Billy to bed. He was so excited having met Mason's buddies and the idea of surfing in the morning, it would be a wonder if he got any sleep at all. Finally Sophia handled things.

"If you don't get to sleep I'll be worried you won't be alert enough to let you surf tomorrow." The words had Billy scrambling towards his bedroom.

Mason followed her into the kitchen where she attempted to start washing one of the pans that was soaking.

"Nope, I told you that's my job. You cooked. I clean."

"Well, we can't leave this to soak overnight," she protested. Mason rested his chin on her shoulder as he looked at the gooey mess made by the apple brown betty.

"Oh yes we can. I'm thinking it needs to soak for a week." God she smelled good. Cinnamon and Sophia—what a combination. He placed a kiss behind her ear and felt her shiver.

"Come on, honey, you need to get to bed too. You're going to come watch us in the morning aren't you?" She turned to look at him, her eyes sparkling.

"I wouldn't miss it for the world. Billy was so excited when we rented the wetsuit for him today. He hasn't done this in forever. This is so great of you." She turned around and found herself in his arms.

"Are you kidding? I love surfing, and it's fun doing it with other people. Billy is so excited about it, I'm going to have a blast."

"But I've seen you surf. You're really going to have to hold back. I appreciate you taking the time to surf at his level."

"I remember the guys who taught me. They had fun doing it just like I'm going to have fun with Billy. It's great seeing it from a newbie's eyes. Also, it never hurts to focus on the basics, it keeps you sharp." He saw the doubt begin to disappear.

"That makes sense. I'm just so happy you're doing this. Mason, you're a good guy. I really liked your friends. They were awfully funny."

"They liked you too. The fact that you baked for them had nothing to do with it." He smiled. "I saw you smuggle a container of chocolate chip cookies home with Clint. There better still be some here for me." He loved seeing her eyes fire and her chin jut out before she realized he was teasing. She was beginning to feel more comfortable with him.

"If you keep giving me a hard time I won't tell you where I put them." He looked around the kitchen, continuing to look at her out of the corner of his eye. Finally he saw her glance at the bread box on the counter. He stepped over and opened it.

"How did you do that?" she asked, her eyes wide with amazement.

"Ancient SEAL secret." He was going to have to talk her into a game of strip poker some time. He opened up the Ziploc bag and took out two cookies as he opened the cupboard. "You want some milk to go with your cookies?"

"Are you out of your mind? How could I possibly eat any more?" Looking at her, he felt she could afford to eat plenty more but he had the good sense not to say it.

"You're not hungry?"

"We just had a huge meal three hours ago with a zillion different desserts. I'm probably not going to be hungry until lunch tomorrow." He grabbed a paper towel and poured some milk and sat down on one of the stools at the island.

"Come here," he said holding out his hand.

"Huh?"

"Come sit on my lap." Mason encircled her good wrist and pulled her inexorably closer until she was standing beside him. Then he lifted her and set her gently on his lap. She wrapped an arm around his shoulder. It felt good.

She didn't say anything just snuggled closer her head underneath his chin, as he bit into the fabulous cookie. He offered her a bite and she shook her head.

"You're really missing out," he said, as he finished the last bite. She twined her other arm around his waist.

"I've got a pretty good deal going on right here." Mason wanted to let out a whoop at her admission.

"I noticed you took one of my W.E.B. Griffin books last night. Have you read him before?"

"No. But I was studying history. We were getting into some of the battles of the Civil War and I found those pretty interesting. So I thought his books about World War II would be good too. I didn't know they'd be so entertaining."

"Still didn't stop the bad dreams though did it?" She shook her head, sadly.

"I can't imagine how bad it is for the girl who was in the car. Can you imagine how awful her life must have gotten for her to make the decision to be a prostitute?" Sophia's face was a mask of concern. He hugged her closer, and she let out a deep breath. "I hope the police find her. I told them to call me if they do I want to talk to her."

"I don't remember you saying that when you gave your statement at the hospital."

"They called today." She looked at him with a look of apprehension. "I meant to talk to you about it."

"Okay."

"I forgot until now." She seemed nervous.

"Honey, with everything going on today no wonder you forgot to tell me."

"The men who did those things. Well, they got out on bail and they can't find the girl. They said your testimony isn't going to be enough so I'm going to be their big witness. They said I have to meet with the D.A." He could see she was upset by everything she'd said.

"What has you most afraid?" he asked as he stroked from the nape of her neck down to her lower back. She didn't answer, and he watched as she gathered her thoughts and courage. He continued stroking, up and down and then back up again.

"I worry for the girl, she seemed so young. But I didn't see her like you did. Was she young?" He thought back to those horrific moments and he saw them all clearly. The girl screaming and running up to him, begging him to call the cops, all but dragging him to the car. Sophia was right she'd been young, probably just out of high school if he had to guess. But as soon as he'd seen those men on top of Sophia his entire focus centered on her.

"You're right she was young and I worry for her too, honey. But there's more than just that. What else has you nervous?"

"It's stupid."

"Is it about those men being out of jail? Because it sure as hell makes me mad."

"But it makes sense. It should make you mad. It should make me mad." Both of her hands gripped his shirt.

"Ah, baby." He shifted so he could look into her eyes. "Are you afraid those men can find you?"

"Can they?" she asked in a hushed voice.

"I don't think they tell your identity until the D.A. has to tell the defendant's lawyers. When do you meet with the D.A.?"

"They want me to come in this week or early next week." He hated the defeated sound in her voice.

"We'll go together."

"We will?" She looked at him with a hopeful expression.

He smoothed her hair. "Yes we will."

"Damn, I forgot. They need to take your statement too."

"I would have gone whether they needed my statement or not." He bent and brushed a kiss against her forehead. He wasn't quite sure how it happened but from now on when Sophia Anderson needed something he was going to do his damnedest to provide it.

* * *

They left the house while it was still dark and drove north on the Five Freeway up to San Onofre. Mason checked and the surf was going to be perfect for Billy, who hadn't been on a board for over three years.

When they got to the beach Billy ran way in front of them. Sophia wasn't worried because she'd heard the rules Mason had laid out. Billy stood up straight, listened intently, and nodded to everything Mason had to say. One of the big no-no's was going into the water without Mason watching. There was absolutely no doubt he led men in the military.

"He's a good kid. You've done a great job with him."

"What? What are you talking about?" Sophia asked, genuinely perplexed.

"You've really been a mother to your brother for quite a while and he's a great boy. I really like him." Sophia blushed.

"I do too. I can't wait for the day he can move in with me." She'd been toying with the idea of getting another job on top of the one at the diner so she could save up faster for the apartment. She mentioned it to Mason.

"What are you thinking of doing?"

"During my sophomore year of college I had a job as a paid intern at a call center for a cable company. I would need to find another job with even more of a swing shift."

"How many hours a week are you thinking of working in total?" Mason asked. He helped her down a particularly rough spot on the trail.

"No more than seventy to save up the money. Then I would have to cut back to fifty when Billy came to live with me." They were at the beach and the sun was just peaking over the horizon. Billy set her blanket on the first table available in a haphazard manner. She laughed. When she looked at Mason to see if he found it amusing, he looked dark and forbidding.

"What's wrong?" Sophia almost lost her footing, unused to seeing that kind of expression on his face.

"I want to talk to you about your work schedule idea after we drop Billy at the Bard's." Sophia's tummy fluttered.

"Well okay." Then she thought through what he'd said. "You have to work I'm going to drop him off by myself."

"I took the day off and we're dropping him off together," his tone brooked no argument. He helped her sit on the table with her feet settled on the bench. She had a thin coat she'd brought when she had packed to go to Mason's, and she wrapped it tight around herself. Mason dropped a thick coat over her shoulders. She looked up in question.

"It's mine. I knew you didn't have one. It's big enough to act as a blanket so you should stay warm." He smiled at her. Sophia snuggled into the shearling coat. Even though it was April in California, dawn at the beach was damn chilly.

"Okay you guys, I expect to be impressed. I brought my phone so I'm going to be taking pictures." And with that, the two of them were off. She watched as they raced towards the water. Billy ran at a manic pace Mason could have easily surpassed, but he kept at Billy's side. That's how the entire morning progressed. Mason would keep a keen eye on Billy's abilities and slow his pace to match. She watched him lean over and provide pointers.

There were a few times Billy rode the waves and it was a wonderful sight to behold. After two hours they came in for a break. Sophia had juice and breakfast burritos ready for them. They ate and rested for a while before they went back into the water. Billy came out and then they both watched Mason surf.

Finally there was a huge swell and he rode a big wave.

"Look at that, Soph, that's rad." Billy even stopped midway from finishing a piece of pie to comment. Rad wasn't the word she was thinking more like magnificent. Especially now that she knew what was hidden beneath the wetsuit.

Mason stayed out for another half hour before he finally headed in. He flopped down beside Billy and looked over at the basket of food and then at her.

"Did Billy leave anything?"

"Nope, growing boy. There's nothing left." Her brother laughed.

"She's lying. She made enough for the two of us and three others."

"Now he's lying. I bet my last dollar there won't be anything left."

Mason peered into the basket and pulled out two burritos. "I'm not going to take that bet." He lay back on his elbows and they all lounged about, watching the surfers, the water, and the colors of the sky. By the time they got up to leave the basket was empty.

* * *

The next morning at the diner Sophia was still marveling over the fact that not only had Mason gone with her to the Bard's, he had followed her back to the diner to make sure she made it home safely. What kind of man did that? For God's sake, she was twenty-two, she drove all over by herself she didn't need a keeper. But he hadn't made her feel weak instead he made her feel cared for.

After the breakfast rush, Margie insisted she take a break and they sat at one of the tables near the back. Frannie DeLuca came over from the food pantry as well.

"Spill," Frannie said as soon as the food was on the table.

Sophia knew she was going to get the third degree, so she'd been considering exactly what she would, and wouldn't, disclose. Kisses, she would admit to kisses. She wouldn't admit to having him sleep in the same bed with her. That was just too intimate.

She explained how Mason and his friend Drake helped at the mission.

"You'll love this," her voice filled with glee. "Drake bought enough groceries for at least one day's worth of meals for the entire mission, it was unbelievable."

"You mean the man with the sexy southern drawl?" Margie asked, her eyes wide, as she reached over for the jelly packets.

"I don't know who he is but I say he's the man you should be with," Frannie said emphatically. Sophia blushed.

"Oh no, you should see the sparks fly between her and Mason, Fran. He's the one who rescued her. He's an honest to God knight in shining armor." Margie put her elbow on the table and sighed.

"Sophia, it's about time you caught a break."

"I don't know, part of me is still waiting for the other shoe to drop. I keep pinching myself like it's too good to be true, you know?"

"How's the sex?" Frannie asked, as she bit into her egg white omelet.

"Frannie!" Sophia's cheeks burned at the question. She was immediately reminded of how he comforted her after her nightmare. Part of her wished they'd made love but most of her was thankful they hadn't. It would have been too much, too soon.

"All right I'll give you a pass. But Margie explained the level of hotness and I'm not sure I could have held out."

Margie snorted. "You know damn well you were a virgin on your wedding night, Francesca DeLuca."

"It was a different time," Frannie defended herself.

"I think it's sweet. I wish I would have waited for the right man." Sophia sighed.

"Is Mason the right man?" Margie asked, motioning for Sophia to eat.

"I'm beginning to think so and it scares the hell out of me because God knows I'm not the right woman."

"That fink Lewis sure did a number on your self-esteem. I wish I could meet *him* in a dark alley." Sophia visibly shuddered.

"Fran, what are you thinking bringing that up?" Margie admonished. "Child are you sleeping at all?"

"I slept okay over at Mason's house. I don't know how I'll sleep tonight. I've been having nightmares. I felt safe knowing he was there, you know?" The two ladies looked at one another.

"What?" Sophia asked, the fork midway to her mouth.

"Maybe you should keep sleeping over at his house," Margie suggested.

"No way, I've inconvenienced him enough. I'll see him on Friday and then we're going on a date on Saturday."

"Why are you seeing him on Friday?" Frannie asked.

"We have to go give statements to the D.A." She put down her fork knowing she would have to force herself to eat after thinking about Friday's meeting.

"You let us know if you need anything. I want to know if you have nightmares, all right." Frannie gave her a hard stare. Sophia laughed. Frannie's bossiness no longer intimidated her after having dealt with Mason. Now *he* was a force to be reckoned with.

"Eat up girlie the lunch shift starts soon. I don't want to see you lifting any trays this time."

"But my arm is feeling much better," Sophia protested.

"I don't care. Resting it will help it heal. I don't want to see you ripping open any of those stitches." Margie was probably right. Her arm did kind of throb after carrying some of the larger trays.

"Okay."

"At last she's showing sense. Our little girl is growing up, Frannie."

CHAPTER TEN

"You look beautiful, Sophia." She always looked pretty but now she looked absolutely beautiful.

"Do you need glasses? It's the third time you've said that, Mason. Have you not noticed the bruising on my face? It's green."

"It matches your eyes and it almost matches the color of your suit." It was the suit, hose and heels really doing it for him. When he originally complimented her on the outfit, she immediately told him she bought it at a consignment store. Like that mattered.

He opened the door for her as they entered the lobby of the Hall of Justice in downtown San Diego. He noticed her clenching her fist. He snagged it and brought it to his lips. She looked up at him in confusion.

"You have nothing to be scared of."

"I'm not scared," she said as they got to the elevators. "Well not exactly. I'm nervous. I called and Mrs. Porter said they wouldn't be here."

He knew she was talking about her attackers. It was a damn good thing they weren't going to be there because he would be tempted to murder them. Looking at her poor face and the way she still favored her ribs and shoulder about killed him.

"You really didn't have to come," she said for the fourth time. As soon as she found out the D.A. wanted to speak to them separately, Sophia said she didn't need him to come.

"I wanted to be here." She was clutching his hand tightly, so he thought she needed him with her as well.

When they got to the correct floor, they were ushered into the office of a middle-aged woman named Hannah Porter.

"Thank you for taking time off to come and see me Ms. Anderson. Who is this with you?" The woman was in her mid-forties and exuded competence.

"This is Mason Gault. He's the man who rescued me."

"Lieutenant Gault, I don't have you coming in until Tuesday." Mrs. Porter frowned up at him.

"I'm here to support Sophia."

"I see." Mason knew she did. He could tell very little would get past this woman and it made him seriously happy.

"Lieutenant, you're going to have to wait somewhere else. I don't want to taint your account of the events by listening to Sophia's. There's a cafeteria downstairs," she suggested.

"I'll just wait in the outer office."

"This could take an hour or two," Mrs. Porter warned him.

"That's not a problem, ma'am."

"Very well." Sophia and Mrs. Porter waited as Mason stood and left the office, leaving the two of them alone to discuss her statement. She'd given him an apologetic look as he stepped out of the office.

Mason glanced around the small outer office and took a seat. There was only one magazine and it was about golf. He didn't golf but at least it was something to read. By the time the door opened he'd read it cover to cover. Twice.

Sophia came out red-faced, with her eyes swollen. It was obvious she'd been crying. He looked at Hannah Porter who had an arm around Sophia's shoulder.

"You did really well. We're going to get those bastards. Thank you for coming in today. I'll let you know when the trial date is set. They already have their attorneys."

As Sophia walked two steps forward into the outer office Mason took her into his arms. He couldn't help it.

"Mrs. Porter, did Sophia ask you when you'll be disclosing her information to their attorneys?"

"I will be today. They sent me a request for all of the discovery documentation." Sophia turned in his arms to look at the assistant D.A.

"So the men who did this will have my contact information?"

"Their attorney will. The defendants, Krill and Dooley, will only have your name. Their lawyer is the only one who will have your contact information. He will advise his clients not to get in touch with you because to do otherwise will endanger their case."

"But they could, couldn't they?" she asked. Mason could feel her trembling.

"If they do their bail will likely be revoked until their trial. They won't want to risk it."

"Seems to me that's a little too late," Mason growled.

"We can't violate their rights. We have to assume they'll follow the law."

"You're kidding me right? After what they did?" Mason demanded. He breathed in, trying to keep it together. Sophia was trembling even harder, and he needed to dial it back. He took a deep breath and pulled her closer. "Never mind. Thank you for your time Mrs. Porter we'll take it from here."

As Sophia turned to make her way towards the elevator she stumbled on her heels. Dammit, she was scared and he didn't blame her. She was just a tiny little thing and now it was possible those animals might know where she lived. She was moving in with him that was all there was to it. By the time they were outside and on the way to his truck he had his argument ready to go but she surprised him.

"No Mason," she said before he had a chance to open his mouth.

"What?"

"No, I'm not going to stay at your house." Dammit, her chin was jutting out. She wasn't pulling on her hair either. She was serious.

"They're going to have your address. They know you're going to testify against them."

"You heard her. They'll go to jail until their trial if they try anything. She told me it could take as long as eight to ten weeks before we go to trial. They won't want to risk it. I'm going to be perfectly safe. I'm not moving in with you. I have plans."

"Tell me."

"I'll tell you tomorrow when we go on our date."

"Let's go out to lunch now."

"Just take me to the diner. I'm wiped out. I need a nap." Dammit, she sure knew how to knock the wind out of his sails.

"Okay, but tomorrow night I want to hear all about your plans." When they got into his truck, he couldn't help but admire how her legs looked in the hose and heels. He thought about stealing a kiss but then he looked at the dark circles under her eyes that had nothing to do with her injuries.

"Why don't you see if you can get some sleep on the way up to San Clemente, okay honey?"

"I can keep you company. Anyway, I want to hear about the training you're always doing." She immediately yawned. He suppressed a grin and explained about the physical training he and his team did to keep in shape between missions. He told her three minutes worth of information and she was asleep.

He called the diner on the way to San Clemente and talked to Margie. She was waiting for him when he pulled around to the back. She let him in and he carried Sophia up to her apartment. She never stirred.

"She's exhausted. I know she hasn't been sleeping," Margie said as she slipped off Sophia's shoes and pulled the blanket over the sleeping woman. They left the small apartment and went downstairs.

"Now tell me everything the D.A. said," Margie demanded. She pushed Mason into one of the seats at the lunch counter. "Hamburger?"

"Cheeseburger." Margie called to Peter, the cook, and then rested her elbow on the counter and waited.

"It could be as long as eight to ten weeks until they go to trial and in the meantime their lawyer knows where Sophia lives."

"You've got to be kidding me."

"I'm not," Mason said in disgust. "I tried to convince Sophia to stay with me but her chin jutted out and I lost the argument."

Margie laughed.

"I know the look. Yeah, you were toast. That girl sometimes has more pride than sense. Of course it has gotten her through so many tough times. I can't believe she's managed to stay so positive and nice considering the cards she's been dealt." Margie's voice was filled with admiration.

"Tell me," Mason asked as she set the food in front of him.

"It's not my story to tell." He guessed it wasn't but he was still disappointed she didn't tell him. "She's a hard one to get talking, Margie."

"I know. It's the pride thing. I'll tell you one thing, you'd be lucky to have a girl like Sophia in your life."

"That's what I think too. Now I just have to convince her." He bit into his burger.

"Just know you have people in your court. We're rooting for you." He hoped it was enough. He still had to find out what was behind the walls Sophia had built up.

* * *

It had taken every last ounce of strength Sophia had not to agree to move in with Mason. She was scared and that was the truth. The idea of staying at Mason's house was like a dream come true. He would keep her safe. But she also listened to what Mrs. Porter said. Dooley and Krill were not going to risk their freedom to come after her so she was scared for no reason. What's more there was something far more important to her than her puny fears—Mason's respect.

Sophia wanted a relationship with this man. He might have started out pursuing her but now she ached to be with him. He made her smile. She hadn't felt this good in years, and she wasn't going to ruin it by having him think she was too afraid to handle things on her own. By God, she would prove to him she was worthy of a SEAL! And it started by getting her ass in gear.

She hadn't been on a date for over three years. Not since college. The best outfit she had she'd just worn to go to the D.A.'s office. Then there was the fact that she didn't know where Mason was taking her. Was it out for a pizza and beer? Maybe jeans were appropriate. She just didn't know. She finally gave in and called him.

"So what's the dress code?" she whispered.

"Hello honey, what's your question?"

She loved his voice. It made her melt. She'd never talked to him on the phone before and he sounded smooth, like smoke and aged whiskey. It took her a moment to respond.

"I was wondering what to wear. Where are we going? Is it a jeans night, or something a little dressier?" Sophia winced at her fast delivery.

He paused. "Wear whatever makes you comfortable." Dammit, she knew he was saying that because he was being nice. It meant he planned to take her someplace dressy. Okay, she could do dressy.

"Okay, I will. Six o'clock, right?"

"Yes, I'll see you then." She hung up. She had money in her apartment fund. It was two o'clock. She would head on over to the consignment store. Margie insisted she skip the lunch shift today so she could get ready. She'd argued but now she was glad Margie insisted.

Maybe she could get Frannie to go with her. She'd really like a second opinion, and she was in luck because Frannie was free. But it turned out to be a really bad idea. By the time she got back to her tiny apartment she had spent over two hundred dollars, which was a lot considering the cheap prices at the store. But she ended up with three great outfits and one killer dress she planned to wear that night.

One of the things that still fit from her days in college, before she lost weight, were her shoes. She planned to wear her peacock teal high heels to go with the new rust colored dress she just purchased. The dress even had sheer long sleeves that covered her bandage. She planned to apply some artful make up to cover her bruises. By God, she was doing the full pull. Frannie sat at her little dining room table while she got ready for her date. At five thirty she turned around.

"Well?" she asked nervously.

"You're a knock-out." Sophia turned to look again in her bathroom mirror. She could only see the top part of her dress but it looked pretty good. The make-up covered the bruising pretty well and the way she highlighted her eyes took the attention away from anything the make-up didn't cover.

"Are you sure?"

"I'm positive."

"I don't know why I'm so nervous. He's seen me without make-up. Hell, he saw me the night I was beaten. This shouldn't matter." Sophia pulled at a lock of her hair.

"It's your first date with him." Sophia shrugged her shoulders in agreement, and winced. Truly, she should not do that it hurt. But it *was* her first date with the man, even if she had slept in his arms, and how great had *that* been.

"You're blushing. Is there anything you want to share?" Frannie looked at her with a twinkle in her eye.

"No, there's nothing I want to share," Sophia said with an embarrassed laugh. "Actually, I think it's time for you to leave."

"How about I tell him what time to have you home?" Frannie suggested with a wink.

"How about you not." Sophia gave her a quelling glance.

"Okay, okay, I'm leaving." Just then there was a knock on the door. Sophia groaned.

"Be good," she admonished Frannie. She went to the door and opened it. She was stunned. Mason was wearing a white dress shirt and black slacks. He looked good enough to eat with a spoon. She finally had the wherewithal to invite him in. He didn't move.

"Mason?"

"Yes?"

"Don't you want to come in? I don't think you've met my friend, Frannie DeLuca. She works at the food pantry where I volunteer sometimes." She stepped aside so he could come in, but he continued to stand at the top of the stairs.

"God, you look beautiful." She'd never seen his eyes so dark blue before. She turned around and Frannie was standing behind her.

"Hi Mason, I'm Frannie. Margie and Sophia have told me a lot about you. I hope it's all true." Frannie held out her hand and Mason took it for a gentle shake.

"It's good to meet you, Mrs. DeLuca. They've mentioned you as well."

"Well, I was just leaving."

"So were we. Let's walk you out to your car," Mason said. He let Frannie lead the way and then took Sophia's keys so he could lock her door. He frowned as he checked out the locks.

"What?" she asked.

"I want to install a deadbolt." His face took on that military look.

"I think the lock I have is fine," Sophia said looking at her door.

"Humor me." They followed Frannie to her car and then made their way to Mason's truck.

"Why do you think I need a deadbolt? Is it because of the men who attacked me?" Sophia's voice was steady but she was pulling on a lock of her hair, which meant she was nervous. He pulled her hand away and held it on the seat between them.

"No. I wanted to have one installed even before we talked to the D.A. That is not the best lock, okay?"

"Fine, I'll get a locksmith."

Mason chuckled as her chin jutted out. He decided to drop the subject. He'd just show up with his tools and a deadbolt. Tonight was not for arguing.

"Do you prefer steak or seafood?"

"I like either."

"Don't you have a preference? I mean there is always a nice filet mignon, but sometimes I'm in the mood for a succulent white fish or salmon. What strikes your fancy tonight?" He spared her a quick glance before watching the road again. He could see she was confused.

"But don't you have a reservation somewhere?" Sophia questioned.

"I have two reservations. So you name which you prefer and I'll cancel the other."

"Oh. That's really nice of you. But don't you have a preference?" Damn she was going to kill him.

"Tonight is about you, honey. We'll have another date that's about me. I'll let you cook and bake for me. Okay?"

"That'd be great," she said with real enthusiasm. Whoo hoo, he got another date.

"So which do you feel like tonight, steak or seafood?" he prompted.

"Seafood," she said decisively. He liked that. When she wasn't worried about other people she knew her mind.

He handed her his phone and told her what restaurant to call so she could cancel the other reservation. They made it down to Oceanside and used the valet parking for the truck. The restaurant overlooked the water and he'd asked for a table on the patio under the heat lamps.

"Careful, honey, those shoes are beautiful but I don't want you to trip." He held her hand and kept his other hand at her lower back.

"I can walk in heels," she assured him. He never doubted it but he also remembered her being in the hospital less than a week ago. As beautiful as she looked, he should have said they were eating a casual meal. He really hadn't thought this through. As they were seated at the table she gave him a look from beneath her lashes.

"Stop it," she admonished.

"Stop what?"

"Stop worrying about me. I'm fine. The stitches are healing. The bruises on my ribs are healing and my legs feel great." She opened her menu and nodded at him to do the same.

He let out a breath and smiled. "Honey, you might as well get used to me worrying about you. It's in the job description. I worry about everyone. All of the men you met at my house are under my command. Their welfare is my concern. I certainly don't feel like you're under my command but I will always be concerned about your safety and wellbeing. It's the way I'm wired."

"They're all under your command? I thought they were your friends."

"They are."

"But isn't there a rule about fraternizing or something."

"Nope, we're a team. We all have one another's backs. They're my brothers. From now on they have your back as well."

Sophia let out a laugh.

"What are you laughing about?" He pulled down her menu so he could see her clearly.

"What you just said. That's silly. They don't know me."

"Give me your phone."

"Why?"

"Just give it to me." He knew he was being demanding, but it was important she listen to him when it concerned her safety. She opened her purse and handed it to him.

"What are you doing?"

"I'm programming in my number as well as Drake's. If there is ever, and I mean ever, a problem, and you can't get ahold of me, you call him. He'll be there. Do you understand?"

She gave him a perplexed look. "That makes no sense."

He rubbed his hand through his hair and tried to think of a way to get through to her. "Sophia, do you believe Margie and Frannie are people you can depend on?"

"Sure," she said immediately.

"But you weren't going to call them when you needed a ride from the hospital, why is that?" he persisted.

"I didn't want to inconvenience them. They were both at work."

"From now on I want you to know you come first for me. You come before my work."

He handed back her phone, and she picked up her menu.

"I think we should order." *Dammit.*

"Okay honey, let's see what sounds good." He turned his attention to the specials and tried not to grit his teeth.

"I'm not trying to make you mad."

Which was the only reason he wasn't going to get mad. He realized she wasn't used to anyone watching her six. Therefore she couldn't wrap her head around what he was trying to do. It was up to him to show her what teammates, what friends, what lovers, what loved ones, did for one another.

"I'm not mad, honey, I'm hungry. What are you going to have?"

She chose one of the two specials and he chose the other. When their dinner came, she closed her eyes and inhaled. It was one of the sexiest thing he'd ever seen.

"This is divine. Oh they used tarragon and lemon with just a hint of cilantro. This is going to be so good."

He couldn't wait to see her eat a bite. He was right, watching her eat was sexy too.

They talked about how Billy did on his math test and he was happy to hear he aced it. She asked him more about his life in the military and about his renovations. He definitely noticed how she steered the conversation towards current events and his life. He was certainly willing to follow her lead for the main course. He knew how to bide his time.

Sophia said she couldn't possibly eat any dessert but he ordered the peach cobbler with a full serving of vanilla ice cream on the side.

"So tell me about your plans," he asked smoothly.

"My plans?" she asked as she dipped a spoon in for a bite of peaches.

"Yeah, you said yesterday you had plans that precluded you from moving in with me. I was wondering what they were."

"Oh, I talked to one of my friends who I used to work with at the cable company. She's a supervisor there now. She said she could get me a part time job working four hours a night. It would be right before opening the diner. They need some phone support and they're bringing some of it back to the United States, isn't that great?"

"Where would you be working?"

"Up north," she said slowly as she twirled her hair.

"Up north where exactly?" Mason waited and knew he wasn't going to like her answer.

"Santa Ana." One of the poorest and most crime ridden areas of Orange County. Great, just, great. It took every fiber of his being not to channel Drake Avery. He counted to ten. He counted backwards from ten to one. Finally he asked.

"What are your hours going to be?" He was proud he kept his voice even.

"Midnight to four, which is great because I'll be able to get to the diner by four thirty and have all the baking started and the diner open by five thirty."

"You're not going to take this job," Mason started out reasonably.

"Yes I am. This is a great opportunity. I worked there before when I was going to school. The hours are perfect. I'm going to be able to save up for a good apartment so Billy can come live with me." Her eyes sparkled and she spooned up a huge scoop of ice cream and waved her spoon at him. "I should be able to have my first and last month's deposit in no time. I'm not going to tell Billy in case something falls through, but this is wonderful."

"You didn't hear me. You're not going to take this job." Mason smiled pleasantly. There was no point in ruining a wonderful date or her great mood, but he needed to get his point across.

"Of course I am. I just told you it's perfect."

"Over my dead body are you going to be waltzing around at midnight in fucking Santa Ana, crime central of Orange County. Do I make myself clear?" Fuck, he might as well be talking with a southern drawl. Sophia stared in disbelief. She didn't say a word just stared. The waitress came up and topped off their coffees and brought the check.

"I can't believe you said that to me. Did you just say that to me? Really?" Sophia sounded genuinely aghast. He had a chance to back out and not sound like a total Neanderthal.

"Fuck yeah, I said it to you. There is no way, on my watch, you are going to do this. We'll figure something else out. You need the money to rent an apartment? Fine, I've got it, it's yours. You need a part time job? I'll find you one where it's safe. But there is not a chance in hell you are going to walk around the streets of Santa Ana in the middle of the goddamn night." He scrubbed both hands through his hair. Goddammit, he was pretty sure he now had ice cream on his head.

* * *

Mason was serious. Mason was pissed. Mason had vanilla ice cream in his hair. She stared at him and covered her mouth. He looked horrified. She grabbed her napkin and tried to hold back. She couldn't. She burst out laughing. She was laughing so hard. There he was, serious as a heart attack, planning on loaning her money, finding her a job, doing whatever was necessary to keep her safe, with ice cream in his hair. She had to stop laughing or she'd start crying.

"Sophia. Honey. Are you okay?" Of course he'd ask that. Of course he'd be worried about her. She dipped her napkin in her water glass and leaned over the table to clean the ice cream out of his hair.

"Thank you."

"You're welcome." It had gotten dark and there were just the heaters on and the candlelight on the table, but his eyes looked much darker than normal, almost black. He was so freaking handsome.

"Talk to me, honey. Tell me I'm toast. Tell me you're going to boil me in oil. Just don't shut me out." He looked so worried. At the same time if she said she was taking the job no matter what he thought he wouldn't look worried. He'd look like a marauder. Some man who thought he had dominion over a woman. But as soon as she had the thought she dismissed it. That wasn't true. Mason didn't want to have power over her. He wanted to keep her safe. There was a big difference between a man who wanted to boss you around because of some kind of ego trip, and one who wanted to protect you.

"Sophia? Say something."

"I take it you don't approve of my plan."

He snorted. "You could say that."

"So what's the next part of this date?" she asked.

"What?" Sophia grinned, happy she'd thrown him off guard.

"I asked what is 'stage two' of this date? Or was dinner all you had planned?" She gave him a pleasant smile.

Mason stared at her and then finally responded.

"There was definitely a 'stage two'. I talked to Margie, she said you only had to work lunch shift tomorrow, right?"

"It seems like you and my boss have gotten kind of cozy. First she lets you into my apartment. Now she's telling you my work schedule. Are you sure you shouldn't be dating her?"

Mason blinked. He definitely wasn't sure how to take her teasing. It was obvious he thought he was going to be in trouble for dictating to her about the job and he couldn't figure out her mood. Well good. It was kind of fun to see him disconcerted.

"Nope, I'm dating the one I want to be dating. But Margie is my backup plan." He grabbed her hand, and guided her to his truck. She loved how pampered she felt.

"I thought we could go to a place in the Gaslight district. It's a little bar I know that plays some great live music."

"I'd love that."

Mason was right. The band was top notch and he even managed to find a seat for her at the bar while he stood next to her. At one o'clock he whispered it was time they head home so she could get enough sleep for work. Since she'd been ogling him most of the night she couldn't agree more. When they got on the Five Freeway heading north to San Clemente she was stunned.

"Where are we going?"

"I'm taking you home, honey."

"But I thought…"

"We're going to go out on a few dates and get to know one another, Sophia." She didn't know if she was happy or pissed. She finally decided she was impressed and deprived. He came up to her apartment, unlocked her door, and insisted on checking out the interior of her apartment. Then he kissed the hell out her and left. Yep, definitely deprived.

The next day when Sophia went down to the diner to start work, Mason was there talking to Margie at the lunch counter. Sophia made her way to the hostess stand and started seating customers. When she had the majority of people seated and orders taken she sat next to Mason.

"So did I forget another date?"

"I was going to come install a deadbolt on your door, remember?"

She stared into innocent blue eyes and wondered how often his mother let him get away with things because of that look.

"I called a locksmith, he's coming tomorrow," she lied.

"Cancel him. I bought the lock and brought my tools."

She let out a breath. This was a stupid thing to have an argument about especially when it would be nice to have the added security.

"All right."

He leaned in and kissed her. Her toes curled.

Mason was done before the lunch shift ended and then he talked her into a movie on Wednesday night.

After her shift was finished she went over to the food pantry to talk to Frannie and Tony. She told them about her plan to earn money for the apartment for her and Billy.

"Are you out of your mind?" Frannie exploded.

"Over my dead body," Tony said in a low voice.

Sophia sighed. She had been somewhat excited at the prospect of landing a job with hours that would dovetail with the diner but she knew there was a downside, which is why she didn't tell the DeLucas sooner.

"You know you sound a little like Mason," Sophia complained.

"The man has good sense. Sounds like someone I'd like to meet." Tony slapped the table and smiled.

"He reminds me a lot of you, Tony, back when you were in a uniform." Frannie cupped Tony's face and kissed him on the cheek. He blushed, and turned his attention back to Sophia.

"So what kind of stupid idea is this? Working in Santa Ana in the middle of the night? Hell girlie, it ain't the best place to be working during the day."

"That's not true. Some of it is poor, but some of it's nice." Sophia defended her choice. Tony glared at her and she glared back.

"Fine, I was making generalizations. But still there is gang activity and you're not going work there from midnight to four in the morning and that's final."

"I know. I already decided not to. I'm going to call Shelly tomorrow. But I still need to find something else to supplement the money I'm making at the diner. It's hard to find one that will work around the hours."

"You'll find something. You're amazing. We'll talk to all of our friends, kiddo." Tony leaned forward and pinched her cheek.

"You guys are the amazing ones." She hugged both of the DeLucas.

She left the food pantry knowing she still had a problem to solve. How was she going to get the money for the bigger apartment so she could petition the courts for custody of Billy?

CHAPTER ELEVEN

He was at her door again to pick her up for dinner and the movies. This time he specifically said they were going to his favorite pizza joint so she wouldn't dress up. When she answered the door in khaki shorts and a pink blouse and flip flops he once again lost his shit. She was gorgeous. He knew his mouth was hanging open. He saw women all over Southern California in shorts but she was flipping gorgeous.

"Mason?"

"Give me a moment."

"Yeah, sure," she said, puzzled. "Do you need to come in? Do you want a glass of water? Something?"

"Oh yeah." He slid his hands into the abundance of honey hair, and tilted her head just right so he could go in for the perfect kiss. Her mouth was open, albeit to ask another question, but still it was open and a SEAL always took advantage of an opportunity.

He went questing and soon she was fire in his arms. They stood for long minutes, as he reveled in the feel of her plush lips, and his tongue glided against her soft one. Realizing there wasn't a chance in hell they'd make it to dinner if he continued an instant longer, he wrenched away. She looked as shell shocked as he felt.

"Pizza. Movies," he croaked. She nodded.

"Sweater." She turned and he watched her world class ass sway in the shorts. He told his dick to settle down. He was losing the battle. His hard-on finally went away by the time they made it to the pizzeria. Thank the Lord.

They ordered and he found out she was a girl after his own heart—she liked the works on her pizza. They talked about all the different characters who were regulars in the diner—surfers, and a lot of guys from Camp Pendleton. He wondered if they were all blind.

"Seriously, they haven't been asking you out?" he asked incredulously.

"Oh they're just big flirts. They aren't serious."

"Honey, they're serious," he assured her. Then he decided he better shut up. He didn't want her to start thinking of playing the field.

"If I'm going on dates with you I would *never* start going on dates with someone else." God, she was a mind reader. "But you're totally wrong. They haven't been serious."

"Okay, honey." And like mana from heaven their pizza arrived. They were halfway through the food when he asked her the question he'd been dying to ask.

"What happened with the job offer?" If she was still intent on taking it, they were going to have skip the movie.

"I turned it down. I thought about what you said and I talked to the DeLucas. They were just as adamant that it wasn't a good idea. I think I knew deep down it was a stupid idea. To tell you the truth, I was scared after what happened in San Diego but I didn't want fear to run my life, you know?"

He took her hand. She looked so forlorn sitting there. He let go and got up so he could sit beside her. "Scooch over." He put his arm around her and kissed her temple.

"I know about trying to conquer your fears. A little over five months ago I lost men on a mission."

"Oh Mason, how awful." She snaked her arm around his waist.

"On the next mission I couldn't get it out of my mind. I was second guessing every decision I made. I just couldn't shake it." He thought about Larry especially.

"What happened?"

"Drake happened. In his normal tactful manner he told me to pull my head out of my ass and start acting like a team leader."

"So you understand why I have to conquer my fears," she said excitedly.

"There's a difference, honey. My career is to lead men into dangerous situations. It's what I'm trained for. Either I do it, and do it right, or I pack it in. Do you really need to put yourself in situations where you are in parking lots in the middle of the night?"

"No, I decided I didn't. But now I'm scared for you."

"I have to tell you, I have one of the best teams there is," Mason said with utter confidence.

"Then why did people die five months ago?"

"It was a bigger job than normal and they sent us in with some newer recruits. They made mistakes that cost lives." It still happened on his watch and he would have to live with it for the rest of his life. But like Drake said, he also learned things, and it would make him a better commander.

"I've also had to see a counselor about this. It really helped me get my head on straight," he said. "Have you seen anyone?"

"No," she shook her head, the blonde silk brushing his cheek.

"I think you should."

"Margie has been bugging me to go, too." Sophia half-heartedly picked at the pizza crust on her plate.

"Margie is a wise woman. Come on, we don't want to miss the movie." He took the crust out of her hand and popped it into his mouth.

* * *

It was eleven o'clock by the time they got back to her apartment. She was grinning ear to ear.

"So you like the works on your pizza and you like Marvel Comics movies. You're perfect, Sophia Anderson."

"I love kick ass heroes and outrageous bad guys. I love all the effects. What's not to love? Any movie where Stan Lee makes an appearance I'm there." She was glowing. He loved those movies as well and the fact she tugged his sleeve and pointed at Stan Lee made him grin.

"Do you want to come in? I can make you some coffee before you drive back to San Diego, or some cocoa if it's too late for coffee." And here he'd been wondering how he was going to finagle his way in for another kiss or two.

"Probably cocoa, I have to be at the base early so I need a good night's sleep."

"Me too, I have to be in the diner by four thirty to start the baking." She unlocked the door and let him in. He was still amazed how she made such a small apartment look so homey and not cramped.

Instead of using a packaged drink mix, she actually heated up milk and added chocolate. They sat at her small table and sipped the drink. "Mason, thank you so much for tonight, I had a great time."

"So did I."

"I was hoping it didn't have to end." She immediately put her cup up to her lips so it covered her expression, but nothing could hide the blush creeping up her face. He waited until she set down her mug, then took her hand in his.

"I've replayed the other night at my house a thousand times, and having you come apart in my arms was one of the highlights of my life. But I've kicked myself ever since."

"Why?" she asked, sounding dismayed.

"That came out wrong," he rushed to assure her. "What I meant was, it was too soon after what happened. You didn't need me touching you."

"It was exactly what I needed. Being in your arms helped me feel good and it chased away those fears. It's why I could finally sleep. Tonight I want more."

"Are you done with your cocoa, honey?"

"I can't drink anymore. I'm too excited. I want you. I've wanted you ever since I saw you in those boxer briefs." He grinned.

Mason looked at the curve of her face. God, she was beautiful and then he saw her chin jut out slightly. He realized he was finally dealing with a woman who knew her own mind. It still killed him she had these crazy notions she wasn't good enough, but he was so damn glad to see her reaching out for what she wanted. He was so impressed with the woman in front of him. Then he had a flashback to her lying in his arms, and despite her determination of the moment, he knew they were going to do this his way. He got up and walked around the table as she stood. "You have to promise me something."

"Anything." Her voice was little more than a whisper.

"If something scares you you'll tell me." She gave him a solemn nod.

They drifted over to the futon and he took her into his arms. It had been hours since he kissed her. God, she tasted wonderful. He was never going to get enough of this woman. He was in deep. Over and over he took and plundered. She rubbed her hands against the scruff on his cheeks. He could tell she liked the feel. For once she was the one to break the kiss and then looked up into his eyes.

"Hurry, I need you so much." Sophia tugged at his T-Shirt, and he allowed her to pull it over his head. She pressed an open mouthed kiss to his right nipple and he hissed with pleasure. She tongued him and then bit him, while he palmed the back of her head his hand massaging her scalp. She whimpered.

"Good or bad honey?" he asked as he loosened his hold in her golden hair. She slid upwards until her lips met his.

"So good." It was all he needed to hear. He pushed down gently on her shoulders ever aware of her injuries, until she was seated on the futon and then knelt between her legs. He had the first three buttons of her blouse undone when she grabbed his hands.

"The blouse stays on."

"What?"

"I don't want you to take off my shirt." He was back on the street in San Diego with her head in his lap. Even then he'd seen bruises beginning to form where those bastards had touched her.

"Are you scared Sophia?" He didn't want to do anything to frighten her.

"No, I'm not scared. Well, except you won't like what you see. I hate the marks they put on my body."

She was looking straight at him, and her eyes were dry. "I was there honey. I saw everything. I don't want anything between us when we make love."

"I can't stand to look. I don't look. The bruises are so ugly I keep a towel over myself when I get dressed so I don't have to see."

His heart was breaking.

"You're beautiful, Sophia. I'm going to prove it to you. Let's see together." She released his hands as he was talking.

"I was there remember?"

She nodded as he continued to unbutton her blouse. He slowly reached behind her and undid her bra holding her gaze the entire time.

"You're the most beautiful woman I've ever known." He pulled the straps down her arms and the cups of her bra fell into her lap. Her eyes welled with tears and dripped down her face. He kissed them away.

"Can we look now?"

She nodded. The bruising was deep and it must still hurt but her breasts took his breath away. They were round and pink tipped and he longed to touch them, to kiss them, to taste them. He said all of those things out loud.

"Really?" she asked in quiet amazement.

"Honey, I just don't ever want to hurt you. But please, I'm dying here. Can I kiss you?"

"Oh yes," she breathed. He inhaled her. Apricots and Sophia. Then he gently kissed and licked every single bruise. She began to pant. His girl liked having her breasts touched. Her right nipple wasn't bruised so he laved and sucked. This time she grasped his head and pulled him forward. Not one to leave a job undone he sucked harder, gazing upwards to gauge her level of passion, and then used the edge of his teeth. She shrieked his name.

"Mason, again." He licked and then gave her the gentlest kiss he knew how. He brought her down slowly. He didn't want to lose his head with breast play.

"I wanted more." She pouted.

"I have other places I want to explore." Mason kissed further down and cursed the fuckers as he reached the bruising on her ribs. He unfastened her khaki shorts and pulled them off along with her panties. Too fast. Too eager. He took a deep breath. He parted her legs slowly devouring the sight of her glistening seam that was slowly opening to his gaze. He spread her further and she flowered open, a pink delight that was his to taste. He couldn't wait. The scent of her was driving him wild.

"Mason?" She sounded shy and hesitant. How could a woman, who was offering him such treasure, sound insecure?

"Mine." He brushed his tongue through her juices, the taste exploding in him. More, he needed more. He was greedy. He could keep this up for days. He brought his fingers into play needing to feel her pussy pulse around him as he suckled her clit. His girl might be shy, but her clit was proud and stiff and wanted attention. He circled it with his tongue, teasing and scraping with his teeth. She shoved herself into his face and he thought he'd won a prize.

"Mason! Do something, now!" The lady made a request. Who was he to deny her? So carefully, very carefully, he took her between his teeth and sucked. She screamed, and her pussy clamped around his fingers so hard he thought he might lose circulation. That's okay, he was a SEAL he could handle it. He pushed up, rotating, stroking, and she screamed again. Her cream gushed and he licked. It took forever for his heart to stop racing. When he looked up she was lying there and staring at the ceiling with a bewildered expression on her face.

He got off his knees, picked her up, and settled her in the center of the small futon. The he lied down next to her and pulled up the comforter.

"Honey, can you tell me what's wrong?"

"Mason, somehow you're helping to put the pieces back together."

* * *

Sophia always woke three to five minutes before her alarm. She didn't know how but she'd always been able to do it. Her mom said she was blessed with an internal alarm clock. Her eyes popped open. She yawned, but didn't stretch. She gloried in the heat and feel of having Mason next to her. He must have stripped down to his briefs in the middle of the night because she had the gift of flesh meeting flesh. It would have been better if he'd been naked. She so needed to seduce him out of his clothes!

She hadn't had any bad dreams. This was only the second time since the night in the alley. This was also the second time she'd slept in Mason's arms. She was pretty sure there was a correlation.

"Do you want me to turn off the alarm before it rings?" She almost jumped out of her skin at the low rumble of his voice.

"How come you're awake?"

"You woke up so it woke me up."

"But I didn't stretch or anything. How did I wake you up?" That was so weird.

"Honey, your breathing changed," he explained. Yep weird, he must get that from all of his training. She reached over and turned off the alarm.

"I'm sorry I don't have time for...you know." Damn, how did you tell a guy who was all warm and snuggly and hard that you had to get to work?

"I understand. What's more I still think it might be too soon for you."

"You don't get to decide." She pushed away from him, wishing she could see him in the dark. "You make me feel safe. I want you. A lot. I just have to go and bake and get ready to open the diner."

"I have to get ready to drive down to the base in San Diego."

"Do you have time to stay so I could at least feed you before you go?"

He groaned.

"What?"

"I'm remembering the taste of you." *Oh my Lord, could your entire body blush?* He pinched her ass.

"Come on, I want a cinnamon roll." He threw back the covers and bounded out of bed like a true morning person. She pulled up the sheet.

"Ah honey, it's still mostly dark and even if it wasn't seeing you naked is one of life's pleasures." She thought back to the night before and got out of bed. Even in the half-light she saw his warm smile. He gave her a kiss and stroked her breasts with the back of his knuckles. She trembled.

"Okay, you get first shower. I'll meet you down in the diner? I don't suppose you have an extra toothbrush?"

"I'm afraid we'll have to share. Can you handle my cooties?" He laughed.

"I *love* your cooties, Ms. Anderson."

Sophia hustled into the bathroom and closed the door. She'd looked at herself in the mirror the first morning after coming home from the hospital but not since. She traced the bruises. They weren't nearly as painful or ugly and they were just bruises. She thought back to Mason kissing her breasts and the things he'd said. She looked up and saw the dreamy look on her face.

"Work girl. You have to get to work." Despite her pep talk she still took longer in the shower than normal, her body felt languid, and she enjoyed the feel of the water pouring over her. She was horny. Mason was wrong. She needed sex, and he damn well better deliver soon.

She was always fast when she got ready in the mornings and today was no different, except for the long ass shower. She brushed her teeth, put her hair in a ponytail, put on her mascara and lip gloss, and wrapped the towel around her so she could grab some clothes from her dresser.

"Damn, you go in without clothes and come out in a towel. No fair." Mason eased closer for a kiss and pulled off her towel. He bent and she lifted, trying to get as close as possible. Through the haze she was aware he was holding her gently, cognizant of her injuries, and she never felt safer or more loved. At that last thought she pulled away.

"Work, I have to get to work."

"Is something wrong?"

"The baking won't get done by itself. I'm going to leave my key on the table and you can come down. We can have breakfast together."

Taking the key off her ring, Sophia scurried out the door. She couldn't get to the diner fast enough. What the hell was she doing thinking about something as silly as love for God's sake?

She pulled the cinnamon rolls out of the fridge and poured the warm water into the pans and set the cinnamon roll trays in the pans of warm water in the oven, knowing the dough should rise in about thirty minutes. Then she started on the banana bread and the blueberry muffins.

She was surprised Mason took so long to come down. The rolls and muffins were just coming out of the ovens. He looked preoccupied and then he smiled at her.

"What are those smells? My God, I think I just went to heaven."

"Oh you don't have to compliment the cook you're going to get plenty. Now that you're here, I'm going to start the omelets." Turning to the stove, she poured the mixture into the pans. She was hungry and worried.

She pulled out the food and put it on the counter. Looking at the time, she knew they had twenty minutes before the diner was set to open. "What's wrong?"

"We just got new orders. We're leaving this afternoon." Sophia's heart skipped a beat and then she felt it just stop.

"How long will you be gone?" She put down her fork knowing she wouldn't be able to eat.

"A week, maybe two, it all depends." He bit in to the omelet and hummed. "My God woman, I love the way you cook. Did you sauté the peppers?"

"Huh?"

He reached out and stopped her from twirling her hair.

"I asked if you sautéed the peppers. This is phenomenal." He took another bite, savoring the flavor.

"Uhm, yeah I did. I'm glad you like it."

He continued to eat and watched her. Finally he spoke again. "I'm sorry I told you about the mission that went to shit. We've been on three that went fine since then. Like I told you, we had some new recruits with us and now we're going with just us it's going to go like clockwork. You've met most of the team. They know what they're doing."

"Who haven't I met?" She looked down at the eggs and all she saw was a mass of congealed mess. She'd gag if she tried to eat.

"Finn Crandall has been on leave. His granddad had to be put into a nursing home so he was home with his mother helping out."

"Oh, that's so sad," Sophia said on automatic pilot.

Mason looked at his watch. "Come with me." He grabbed her hand and pulled her into the kitchen. Leaning back against the counter, he pulled her between his legs and she rested against him. He didn't kiss her. He just hugged her and stroked her hair.

"I've never had someone to come home to before. Sure I've had my parents but you are fast taking over my every thought. I think about your sparkling eyes, your beautiful smile, and I just can't wait for the next time I see you. I'm coming back to you. I promise." He breathed the words into her hair. Just holding and rocking her.

Once again making her feel safe and loved, which still scared the crap out of her. The idea of being loved by Mason Gault brought tears to her eyes. Because once he realized how needy she was, just like her dad and others said, he would want to leave.

But more than that, so much more than that, was the overwhelming need for him to stay safe. He had to stay safe. She grabbed him closer, wincing as she pulled the stitches in her shoulder.

"Honey, I've got to go."

"Wait a second." She ran over to grab a big plastic container and a smaller one. Mason's face broke into a greedy smile.

"Cinnamon rolls?"

"You have to promise to share. I don't want you all tired for your mission," she teased. "The bowl has the icing and it tastes better if you put it on right before you serve them." He just shook his head.

"Sophia, I'm not quite sure you've figured out who you're dealing with, but okay." He held the treats as she walked him to the back door, close to where he parked his truck.

"I probably won't be able to call you."

"I figured." She felt hollow knowing how much she would miss him.

"Depending where we are I might be able to access my messages. Would you leave me some?" he asked as he stroked her cheek. She turned and kissed his fingers.

"Of course." She couldn't imagine what she would say but she would honor his request. He gave her a precious kiss and then was gone. She locked the door behind him not knowing how she was possibly going to get through the day. She didn't know how she was going to survive until he came back.

Please God, take care of him.

CHAPTER TWELVE

Finn looked like he had been wrung through a ringer. They were due to leave in five hours. Mason took him aside to see if the man's head was on straight before they went into the field.

"It was awful, Mase. I was home just last year for Christmas and Grandpop was rock solid. But really it wasn't so much him I was worried about. Seriously, he didn't recognize Mom or me. He didn't even realize he was going into assisted living. It was how it was tearing Mom apart that killed me."

Mason thought about his grandfather on his dad's side. He might not get around well, but he had all his faculties and he was great to be around. He was in a nursing home, but he had his own apartment and he loved it there. He had tons of friends and it was close to where his parents lived. But Grandpa just becoming a shell? He couldn't imagine it.

"How is your mom holding up?"

"Not good. I think I have her convinced to move out here."

"How about you?"

"I just keep picturing it being Mom, and it's freaking me out. I've been having bad dreams about it. As soon as we get back from this mission, I'm going to go see the doc." Mason smiled. This was why he loved the men on his team. They had their shit together. Finn realized he had a problem and was going to do something about it.

"So are you going to be good for this little outing?"

"Yeah, my head's going to be in the game. But I was wondering about you," Finn said looking him in the eye.

"What about me?" Mason asked genuinely puzzled.

"I hear you're pretty twisted up about some girl."

"I take it there has been some gossiping going on."

"Well what the hell else were we going to do while we were eating homemade cinnamon rolls?" Finn laughed.

"Twisted up isn't the right term. She's amazing. Did they tell you what happened to her?"

"Yeah, and how you came in like a knight in shining armor. Are you sure this isn't some kind of rescue fantasy? I know you, you definitely want to go and save the western hemisphere." Finn watched him as closely as he'd been monitoring him a few minutes ago.

"Let me tell you something about her. There she was, in my arms, beaten and bloody, and she was asking about the other girl wanting to know if she was safe and sound. Then when we're at the hospital, even though she's in pain and made to wait, she's cracking jokes. She's not any bigger than a minute and she's positive she can take care of everyone else including me. Hell, she can spot Stan Lee in a movie before I can."

Finn burst out laughing.

"I've got to meet this woman."

"You'll love her." Mason paused and looked at his friend with the dimpled chin and rugged good looks. "You'll love her like a sister."

"I'm hearing you loud and clear, buddy." Finn winked.

* * *

Sophia looked at her phone like it might grow tentacles. Why was this so damn difficult? *Because I don't like leaving messages.* Sophia knew this was an old phobia leftover from the dad days. But Mason wasn't like her dad and he'd asked her to leave a message, so she was going to grow a set and leave a freaking message. She still sat on her futon and stared at her phone.

She took a deep breath and then her phone rang. It was an unidentified caller. But she'd talk to anyone at this point to get out of calling Mason's phone.

"Hello, this is Sophia."

Nothing.

"Hello?"

Nothing.

"Can I help you?"

She hung up the phone.

"Okay, that didn't work out so well." She pressed Mason's contact number and it went straight to voicemail. She had her message planned.

"Hi Mason, it's Sophia. Margie says hi and so does Billy. I saw him on Sunday and he really hopes he can go surfing with you again soon. I'm still looking for another job. I'm scouring the want ads but so far I haven't found anything you and the DeLucas will approve. I uhm, I uhm. Well this is the part where I tell you I miss you. It's really the truth dammit. How the hell do I know you for less than ten days and miss you so much. It makes no sense. So I miss you and you have to take care of yourself because I need you to come back like you promised. And now I have to be done with this message. Come back because I miss you. A lot."

She hit end fast and then burst into tears. She'd seen his body. He had a fucking bullet wound under his left arm. He said it was a flesh wound but it was an honest to God bullet wound! This man and his friends did things people in movies did only for real. She needed him back home. She picked up the pillow he'd slept on. She hadn't washed the pillowcase since doing laundry. She didn't want to lose the scent of him.

"Please, please be safe Mason. I'm falling in love with you but I don't care about me. You're too important not to be safe. Please be safe. Please be safe." She kept saying it over and over again into the pillow.

* * *

Another fucking jungle. It was the first jungle they'd been back to since Larry died. They'd already been there for three days. They were only four miles away from the target they'd been prepped to take out, and then he got word they needed to head thirteen miles due south and do a rescue mission instead. "Gather the team, will ya?" he asked Drake.

"Jesus, is it that bad?" Drake asked.

"Worse," Mason answered. "Worse squared and then cubed." Drake went to grab the men.

As soon as everyone was circled, he looked at his men and felt a huge surge of pride. "Gentlemen, I want to welcome you to the jungle and tell you that all of your studies and briefings don't mean jack shit."

"Cool, I forgot to do my homework." Clint grinned.

"How bad?" Finn asked.

Mason flipped his satellite laptop around and started walking them through their new mission plan.

"Christ on a cracker! I only packed my spinach. I didn't pack Iron Man's suit," Drake muttered.

"Tennessee boy has turned into a pussy while I was on leave." Finn laughed.

"Hell, on this one I want the suit and Thor's Hammer. Instead I'm stuck with the four of you assholes." Everyone laughed, just liked Mason wanted them to.

Darius, ever the voice of reason, pointed to the screen. "It almost looks like nothing more than a shack. I'm only seeing two guards. Is that right?"

"According to the e-mail this came with yeah, that's the way I'm reading it too, but in about an hour we're going to get more intel and another set of satellite photos."

"Okay, let's get a move on." Everyone hoisted their gear and started out on a good clip towards their new targets—a family who needed to be saved.

In precisely three hours, they gathered because the new information came across and it wasn't good. They had until dark before the family was going to be videotaped while they were being killed. Apparently the father worked for a drug lord and was an informant for the DEA. This public reprisal was to stop anyone else from wanting to do the same kind of thing in the future.

Clint had things figured out down to the second. They would need to run flat out for the next forty minutes to make it there in time. Then they would have thirty minutes to scope out the situation. Darius would be allowed slack since he was the medic and they would need him more rested. He would also be monitoring incoming intel to determine if anything new was on the horizon.

"Move out," Mason yelled.

They made it in thirty-seven minutes. There were still only two guards outside the shack. It was light, no infrared goggles were needed, and Clint, Drake, Mason and Finn each took a side of the building and closed in. Clint and Finn quietly took out the two guards. Mason and Drake made their way into the shack and found four people bound and gagged. There was an older couple and two women in their late teens or early twenties. All of them were in bad shape. By the time they had them untied Darius was coming through the door.

"Darius, come over here mine's bad," Clint said.

"I'll be there, but we have to be gone exactly at sunset that's twenty minutes otherwise we'll be overrun."

Darius went over to one of the younger women. The back of her dress was shredded. She'd obviously been whipped. When they took off her gag she started screaming. Mason couldn't blame her but they needed her to be quiet.

Clint was talking to her in Spanish and telling her everything would be all right, that they were here to rescue them. But she wasn't listening.

Mason was working with the mother, and Finn untied the father who went over to the screaming daughter and got her settled so Clint could put her over his shoulder. It was going to be a long night. Hell, it was going to be a long five days to get them to the evac point.

* * *

"So what's with all the crank calls?"

"What are you talking about, Margie? Nobody's been calling the diner." Sophia tucked her order pad into the waist of her shorts and made her way back to the kitchen.

"Girl, I'm talking about the hang-ups you've been getting on your phone."

"Oh those." Sophia dismissed her question as she handed Peter her orders. "Those are just wrong numbers."

"You've had the phone for how long?" Sophia placed plates on a tray knowing Margie would answer her own question when she didn't she looked up. "Answer me, how long have you had the number?"

"Since college."

"So for five years. How many wrong numbers have you had?" Sophia tried to remember. "For God's sake Sophia, think it through. You've probably had as many 'wrong numbers' in the last week as you've had in five years." Sophia put down the tray and stared at the woman. She was right.

"You really didn't notice, did you?" Margie's tone gentled as she realized Sophia hadn't been ignoring the issue.

Sophia shook her head.

"It's Mason, you're not thinking worth a damn. Have you heard from him since he left?" Sophia shook her head again.

"That's a good thing. You would have heard something if there'd been a problem. He'll be back in no time. He said one or two weeks, right?" Sophia nodded. She was beginning to feel like there was a string attached to her head. She cleared her throat.

"He's been gone for nine days."

"Frannie, Tony, and I were talking about getting together for a game of cards tonight. You interested?"

Sophia nodded but then caught herself.

"That would be great," she said in a husky voice.

"Okay, let's get these folks watered and fed and kicked the hell out. Are you much of a poker player?"

"A couple of guys in college tried to teach me but I never really got the hang of it. It didn't make sense that you would lie."

"Bluff, it's called bluffing. You really need to learn." The older woman laughed.

It took them two more hours before the diner was closed and cleaned which was right when Tony and Frannie showed up.

"What are the stakes?" Tony asked Margie.

"Same as always."

He rubbed his hands together.

"Does she know?" he pointed at Sophia.

"You explain it to her."

Sophia looked around the table. Frannie was innocently shuffling a deck of cards.

"Sophia, we play for food. I usually win. It's great. I get the meals of my choice and these beautiful women have to cook for me."

"Seems like a lose/lose situation," Sophia countered. Frannie looked up from dealing.

"You're wrong. His eggplant parmigiana is to die for. Occasionally he does lose and he makes that and cannoli and Margie and I are in heaven."

"Very impressive." Sophia tilted her head at Tony with a smile.

"They were my mama's recipes. But I rarely lose. I'm looking forward to you baking me many treats. Do you know how to bake pumpernickel bread?"

"Of course she does," Margie said batting Tony in the back of the head. "If it can be baked in an oven then it can be made by Sophia Anderson. Deal the cards, Frannie. Sophia, we're going to play the first four hands to teach you. These bets won't count."

Tony gave each of them a roll of nickels. "At the end of the game the person with the biggest pile of nickels gets to request the food they want from the other people. Should I place my orders now?"

"Shut up, Tony," the two older women said in unison. Sophia laughed. It was the first time in nine days she was starting to feel relaxed.

It took the better part of three hours for Sophia to win the majority of the nickels on the table. It was easy. Everybody always assumed she was bluffing when she bet high and they never folded. However, she was really lucky that night and had good cards so she won most of the pots.

After the game was over Tony asked her to lie to them.

"I don't understand." He wasn't making any sense.

"It's simple. We just want to see you tell a lie," Margie explained.

"I don't lie very well."

"Try," Tony coaxed.

"Uhmm, Peter makes really good clam chowder." She tried to say it decisively but it came out more like a hesitant question.

"Okay then. Now we know to never assume she's bluffing," Tony said with a satisfied smile.

"Tony, I know what I want from you but what should I ask for from Margie and Frannie?"

"Margie's brisket is out of this world and you have to make sure she provides baked beans and corn bread."

Margie beamed.

"Now my Frannie is one fantastic cook but her best dish is not something I'm going to tell you all about."

Sophia was fascinated by how Frannie's red dye job conflicted with the red that now suffused her face.

"I cook Hungarian Goulash."

"She does and that's the other thing she does that will make you think you've died and gone to heaven."

"Enough! I haven't had a date in three months and her man is out of town. So you two love birds need to tone it down." Margie turned to Sophia. "You're definitely going to be gaining some weight, my dear. When do you want to come over to my son's for dinner?"

"I have a better idea. Can you do it all the same day and bring it over to Mason's house and feed him and his team when they come back?"

"Ah Sophia, that's a wonderful idea," Margie said as she leaned over and hugged her neck. Frannie hugged her from the other side and kissed her cheek. Sophia was sure she had a bright red lipstick mark on her face. She couldn't be happier. At least not until she got the call Mason was home.

* * *

"She's burning up with fever, Mason." Darius sounded desperate. They were in the middle of a monsoon. The rain hadn't let up for three solid days and the lacerations on Lydia's back were now infected.

"The drug cocktail didn't work?" Clint asked.

"To a point. If not for the antibiotics she'd be dead by now. She has two more days tops. We've got to move faster."

"Dare, do you have anything stronger to give her? She's in such pain, it's killing me to hear her. It's not that she's screaming or anything. It's just knowing she's awake and trying to keep it in that's making me want to kill somebody and then dig 'em up and butcher them again." His tone was brutally anguished.

"I'm sorry, Clint, I can't. If I give her anything stronger than what I have she might stop breathing. I can carry her for a while if you want," Darius offered. Clint gave him a cold stone look and Darius shrugged.

"Okay, her dying is unacceptable. We'll move faster," Clint said.

"Clint, if you can't keep up the pace, we can help."

"I'll keep up. Hell, I'll lead if necessary." They broke their huddle and went back to the others intent to get back on course. Mason was carrying Elspeth. She'd been keeping up for the first three hours of the morning but after a while she slowed things down. So now he was carrying her.

"Mason, don't let my sister die," she said in perfect English.

"I won't." It was a solemn vow.

"I'm serious. Out of all of us she's the one with honor. She matters. Those animals did that to her because they knew it. You leave the rest of us behind if you have to but don't let her die." He looked into the woman's fierce black eyes and saw nothing but truth. Fuck, what was it about self-sacrificing women these days? How had he become so surrounded?

"Elspeth, you'll all survive. You need you to keep calm so I can concentrate on getting us the hell out of here." And like God was watching over them, the rains came plummeting down and there wasn't a chance in hell he could have heard anything else Elspeth might have had to say.

Mason wasn't sure how long he kept at it. He just kept staring at the foliage twenty feet in front of him intent on not tripping. Then Drake was there.

"Ease up, Lieutenant. I've set up a place for us to hunker down for an hour. It's twenty minutes ahead." Mason nodded. He ached. Elspeth was a dead weight.

"Tell the others." The Hildalgo family were all either unconscious or too delirious to care what he and his team were saying.

"I'm stunned she's still alive," Darius said baldly. Finn clamped his hand down on Clint's shoulder to keep him from going at Darius.

"Keep it together, Clint, he's telling us what we need to know," Mason bit out.

"When that fever spiked the night before last, I thought we lost her but she made it. I think we're out of miracles though. This rain is killing her. We have twenty hours before we hit our extraction point. We've got to haul ass. We've been moving too slow by letting the mister and missus go under their own steam. We're going to have to carry them the rest of the way." Mason looked around and everybody nodded in agreement.

"I've got the mister," Drake said. It made sense. He was the largest and he could hold the man.

"I should take point then," Finn said. Mason nodded. After Drake, he was the next best scout of the group.

"I've got the missus. Before we go let me check everyone out. Make sure everyone has eaten," Darius said.

"Men, let's make sure we don't fuck up on the obvious. Make sure our charges drink water. I'd hate to think in the middle of a monsoon someone is dehydrated." They all nodded. "We're out of here in five."

Mason pulled out his phone and saw he still didn't have a signal. He didn't think he'd have one, but a guy could hope. Even after nine days of jungle green he was still missing Sophia eyes. It would have been nice to have heard a message from her.

* * *

"Mase, I didn't feel her pulse." Clint's eyes were bright as the huey settled into the clearing.

"She was breathing during our last rest stop. Darius said she was going to make it, Clint. Darius is never wrong." They were the last two in line as the civilians were loaded into the belly of the bird.

"In, in, in." Clint and Mason were already climbing aboard when the door gunner was yelling at them to get on the bird. Clint skidded on his knees to the pallet holding Lydia. They had an IV in her arm. The corpsman working on her gave Clint a thumbs up. Mason could finally breathe. Everybody had come out of the jungle alive this time.

He looked around the belly of the huge chopper and saw men and women tending to the civilians as they took off for the aircraft carrier. Home. He was headed home. Home was now Sophia.

CHAPTER THIRTEEN

It was three in the morning. She was reading another one of the books she'd stolen from Mason's bookshelf and trying to keep the nightmares at bay. The phone rang. She could hear it even though it was in her refrigerator. She stored it there because she wanted to get some sleep and didn't want to be bothered with all of the crank calls she'd been getting. But she'd left it on in case Mason called. She knew she wasn't making any sense but she was so tired she didn't know what else to do. If it was possible to buy a clue she'd purchase four.

She got up and ran to the fridge. She checked the phone display expecting to see an unidentified caller and almost dropped it when she saw Mason's number. She pressed enter.

"Hello, Mason? Where are you?" She was so excited she almost yelled the questions.

"I'm outside."

"Where outside?" She was already running to her door, and throwing the deadbolt. Shit, she was in her sleepshirt, but she didn't care.

"I'm at the backdoor." She flew down the stairs and unlocked the door and there he stood. He looked haggard, but beautiful, in a light blue T-Shirt and cargo shorts.

"You really should have a security chain for this door," he frowned.

"Are you for real?" she demanded as she launched herself into his arms. He caught her and lifted her up to his mouth. It was the hottest kiss she'd ever received. Sizzling. She struggled to keep up. She wrapped her legs around his waist. She heard the door close in a haze of heat. The rhythm of the stairs had her pussy rubbing against his belt buckle. Not at all what she wanted to be rubbing.

Another door, this one slammed shut. Her world tilted as she was lowered to the futon.

"Look at me." He had a beard. God, he looked good. She couldn't help herself, she gripped his cheeks and stroked his beard. Then she scrubbed her cheek against the bristles and gave a deep moan. "I'm looking."

"I can't stop this time."

She gripped his hair and looked him dead in the eyes. "I'll kill you if you stop."

"How's the shoulder? The ribs?"

"I'm fine. I'm healed." She stopped short and pulled his head back even more. She tried desperately to roll over, get on top. It was no use.

"What about you? Are you okay?" He smiled.

"I think you should take inventory, honey." She loved the idea.

"Take off your shirt. Oh hell, just strip," she commanded.

He shook his head. His hands pushed under her already rucked up sleep shirt and pulled it over her head. He looked at her breasts under the glow of the bedside light.

"I've missed your breasts. I thought of them often." After the last time he touched them and kissed them, she'd been able to dress and undress without wincing at her reflection. She felt how hard he was. She saw the fierce light of hunger in his eyes.

"Baby, your nipples are so hard. Do they need some attention? Do they want to be sucked?" *A talker? He was a talker?*

"Yes!"

"Tell me what you want."

"I want your mouth on my breasts."

He licked around her left areola while gently squeezing her right breast. Lick, squeeze, lick squeeze.

"More."

"More what?"

"My nipple," she whined. He grinned. He scraped his beard against the hard flesh of her nipple and she screeched. It almost hurt but it felt so good. His eyes lit up like fire crackers. The bastard knew.

"What honey, want me to suck? Want me to bite?"

She put her hand on top of his and squeezed hard but it had no effect. He was in charge and oh wasn't that sexy?

"Please Mason, stop teasing." She let go of his hand, and cupped his cheeks so she could lift his head and look into his eyes. "It's been too long. I've dreamed of you. Tease later. Please?"

He bestowed the gentlest of kisses on her. So beautiful. Tears leaked. He saw and understood. He got up and stripped.

It was the first time she really got a chance to see him naked. So gorgeous.

"You're the beautiful one, honey. Every succulent inch of you. You're everything I never knew I wanted." More tears leaked. She struggled to sit up but he pressed a hand against her sternum. "Stay down. I need my fill and I haven't tasted you in weeks. Are you wet for me, honey?" He pulled down her panties and knelt between her spread legs. *God, not again. Can I survive him doing this to me again?*

"Mason, if you don't fuck me this time, I swear…"

"Honey, my cock is so saying hello to your pussy tonight. That's going to happen but I *need* this first." His tongue delved deep, and then she heard him swallow and sigh. She blushed to the roots of her hair. But then she was parted and he was making lazy forays leaving her struggling for breath. He lifted the hood of her clit and suckled softly and she melted and blasted into orgasm.

He pulled a condom out of his shorts. She was relieved to see he had to rip it off a strip. He'd come prepared. Sophia hadn't really looked at her last lover's cock. She'd been too shy but she couldn't take her eyes off Mason's. It was compelling and she needed it. She canted her hips, putting her heels onto the edge of the futon.

"No, we're going to do this my way." He lifted her easily and put her into the center of the futon. He put a pillow under her hips and then laid beside her and hugged her.

He kissed her neck, one hand stroking towards her breasts. His mouth followed. Taking his time, his tongue trailed clouds of pleasure from one tip to the other and she writhed and pleaded. Ever downwards, until his fingers parted her, where she provided an even wetter welcome.

"Please now," she begged softly.

"God yes," he groaned.

He rose above her careful to keep his weight on his elbows. Sophia watched their joining. He felt so good and the sensation was heady and lush but she still winced.

"Sophia?"

"More." He stayed still and she willed herself to relax. He pumped shallowly until she was mad with want and pushed upwards impaling herself. *Ow.* He was huge and it had been a while. Maybe slow would have been better.

"Dammit." He slowly withdrew and she felt just as bad. *Make up your mind, Anderson.* She tried to shove up again but he stopped her.

"I need you," she protested.

"You'll get me." He chuckled between gritted teeth. He reached down and smoothed his finger over her clit as he slowly started surging within her. Her breath stopped.

"Breathe baby. You've gotta breathe."

Swoosh. He swelled. She swore he got bigger as he lit up every tingly girl spot inside her and she squirmed and twisted and shifted to get closer. He laughed. He swirled his cock and she squeezed her eyes shut, trying to hold in all the sensations. So close. He drove her relentlessly higher and then she shattered. She heard his groan and she grabbed his ass with her heels and hands determined they be as close together as possible as they hit heaven.

* * *

Mason felt like he'd been caught in a tornado. He looked down at the woman in his arms. He didn't want to move, but he had things to take care of. Then he kissed her and kissed her again.

He walked into the bathroom and disposed of the condom and washed up. When he looked in the mirror he saw the silliest grin on his face. He also noticed he looked like death warmed over. He needed to sleep but his cock thought differently.

He turned to leave the bathroom, and there was Sophia, all warm and beautiful. She wrapped her hands around his waist, and he rubbed against her as she wiggled a welcome. She looked at him with slumberous green eyes.

"I already turned off the alarm clock. We have a half hour and I know just how I want to spend it." She slid down his body until she was on her knees. But things weren't working quite right because he was too tall. He helped her back up and guided her to the futon.

"Are you sure?"

"I'm not really all that experienced but I've noticed hard work and enthusiasm usually helps me succeed at any job I take on." He shouted with laughter.

"Hopefully there won't be a lot of hard work involved, honey."

"Mason, have you seen the size of this thing? There is definitely hard work involved." He laughed some more. She was killing him. Then she had him in her mouth, all hot and wet, and he couldn't think let alone laugh. She was using her hands, and they were small and soft, but it was her mouth that was making him sweat. She gulped deeper, and he groaned. Then all the delicious stroking and sucking stopped. He looked down into startled green eyes.

"God. Please don't stop. Your enthusiasm is working."

Her eyes turned languid and she launched into an orchestrated effort to drive him mad. Her tongue made leisurely forays up and down, around, and around. He worked hard to keep his eyes open and on her. It was worth it. What started out as a lark, was something his woman was clearly luxuriating in. Her cheeks were hollowed, her face flushed with arousal, and her eyes had taken on a dreamy expression. All of it combined with the soul shattering sensations she was invoking, and he was seconds away from detonation.

He settled his hands into the silk of her hair, tugging her away, but she was having none of it. Then suddenly the licks centered on the spot right under the head of his cock and he was a goner. She licked. He trembled. She swirled. He throbbed. She rubbed. He erupted.

They both fell backwards onto their elbows. Barely, just barely, he had the presence of mind to pick up the half glass of juice he had seen on her nightstand and pull himself off the bed and cup the back of her head.

"Here honey, drink this."

"Don't want it," she slurred. He thought back to how he felt tasting her and totally understood. He drank the juice, and then lied back on the bed, wiped out. She got up and wandered into the bathroom, not in a straight line either. He put the crook of his arm over his face. Now he wasn't making love, everything ached. He literally hadn't slept in thirty-six hours, and the only thing keeping him upright had been the thought of Sophia. He willed himself not to sleep, not until he'd seen her come out of the bathroom naked. If she was wearing a towel he'd somehow find the strength to get off the bed and yank it off.

"Mason?" she whispered.

"Mmmm?"

"I'm going downstairs. I'll bring something up for lunch. Let's get you under the covers." He realized he was lying sideways on the futon, with his legs hanging over the side. He rolled onto his stomach and eyed her.

"You have clothes on."

"I promise to take them off tonight," she said with a smile.

Mason closed his eyes. "Good."

* * *

Sophia's arms were trembling as she wrestled the pans out of the oven. She needed sleep. She really couldn't blame Mason since he hadn't shown up until three in the morning and she was still awake. Dammit, she'd only gotten about seven hours sleep in the last three days and she wasn't going to make it. She'd tried taking a nap but the dreams and anxiety left her staring at the ceiling.

As she put the third pan onto the counter the phone rang and she dropped it onto the floor.

"Shit!" She stormed to her phone.

"What?" she asked belligerently.

"Sophia?" It was Margie and she didn't sound well. Well double shit on a cracker.

"Margie, oh my God, I thought you were the crank caller. What is it? What can I do for you? Are you okay?" Margie never called.

"Helen had a miscarriage." Sophia pictured Margie's beautiful and loving daughter-in-law and wanted to cry.

"What can I do?"

"I'm going to have to take care of Todd and Ellis for a while. I was hoping you could take my spot as the manager and supervise Brenda in my absence. You'll have to move her to full time. Be sure she pulls her weight. Don't let that boyfriend of hers hang around too much, he's bad for business."

"Sure, I'll do whatever needs to be done. You take as much time as you need." Sophia could feel actual sweat trickling down her back. Gritting her teeth, she told herself she would just find a way to cope.

"You're a good girl. Frannie bringing you into the diner was one of the best things that ever happened to me. I'll call you tomorrow...or maybe the next day." Sophia heard the pain in her boss' voice and wanted to make it better for her.

"It's all good. I'll say a prayer for Helen." She heard Margie choke back a sob.

"Thank you, dear." Then there was the sound of a dial tone. Sophia looked up at the clock. She didn't have much time. She called Brenda and got her voicemail. *You can do this, Anderson.*

She flipped the open sign and Peter arrived and donned his apron to start the grills. Her regulars were there for their coffee and rolls. It wasn't until about six o'clock that people really started coming in for breakfast. By seven it was a steady stream. At seven thirty Margie and the masses usually arrived but today it was just her. She dropped a tray of food. Walter and old man Cooter gave her a standing ovation, and then they helped her clean it up.

It didn't slow down until ten forty-five which was when she had a chance to call Brenda. It still went to voicemail.

"Sophia, you need help," Peter told her.

She choked back the urge to say 'no shit' but it was a near thing. He must have read it on her face though, because he immediately apologized for stating the obvious. He went over to the small desk Margie used to do the bills and wrote out a HELP WANTED sign and went to the front of the diner and taped it to the window. Sophia smiled.

She went back to the front and started seating people for lunch. She had just delivered what seemed like her eighty millionth cheeseburger when she saw Mason sitting alone in one of the booths. He smiled at her.

"Sophia," Lester shouted from across the room. "You forgot the dill pickles. You know I like extra dill pickles." He was right she did know that. But for goodness sake didn't he notice it was just her? She went over to the window to the kitchen and saw Peter already put up the little plate of pickles. She took them back to Lester and then seated two more parties before going over to Mason.

"I'm sorry I didn't have a chance to bring your lunch up-stairs like I promised."

"Where's Margie?"

"It's a long story. What can I get you?"

"Do you need help?" He surveyed the diner, noting almost every table was full.

"Nah, I've got it." He hesitated.

"Honey, get me whatever is easiest and fastest, okay?"

"You need to order whatever you want," she insisted.

"I said easiest and fastest. Go back and tell Peter exactly that, or…" He got up from the booth. "New people just got here. You go tend to them. I'm going back to the kitchen."

Sophia watched him go. She really didn't have time to try to figure things out, instead she went and seated the next group, and took the orders from the last six people she seated. When she went to the kitchen window to give Peter the order, she saw Mason back there wolfing down a sandwich and drinking a large glass of milk. Peter was busy gossiping like he was at a church social.

"Pete, you got a spare apron I can swipe?"

"Sure thing, you going to go help our girl?"

"Damn right." There was the commander voice again.

"What the hell do you think you're doing? You just got back from wherever the hell you were. You're not going to help out in the diner," Sophia exclaimed, as she shoved open the door to the kitchen.

"Pete, go settle the natives for a second and tell them their waitress is taking five."

"Got it." Pete grinned at the two of them before heading through the kitchen door.

Mason pulled her into the pantry and slid down the wall pulling her with him until she was settled on his lap. He cradled her like a child.

"Honey, you're barely holding it together. How much sleep have you had?" She couldn't get into this with him right now.

"Can we not talk? Can I just rest for the five minutes?" His blue eyes were so tender, she melted. He cupped her head and held her against his heart. Her mind drifted. This felt too good. Too good. She shouldn't get used to this. She was being too needy. Men didn't like it. That was her, Sophia the needy one. She gave a deep sigh and pushed up.

"What's wrong? I mean besides the obvious?"

"Nothing. Nothing's wrong. You don't have to comfort me. I'm not somebody who needs to be comforted at the least little thing. I'm not a wimp." She watched as his face took on an utter look of confusion.

"Honey, you are the furthest thing from a wimp. As a matter of fact, I would love it if you would lean on me more." She snorted. *Yeah, sure.*

"Look, it's the lunch rush I've got to go. You need to go and rest. I'll see you later. I'm so happy you came and visited last night. Thank you for that."

His face no longer looked confused it was fast showing anger.

"You're happy I visited last night?" he asked incredulously. "Let's get the hell out to the diner and feed some people before I blow a gasket. We are going to have a serious talk tonight. This shit has been going on long enough." He jumped up off the floor and took her hand and led her out to the diner.

The lunch hour rush went a lot better with Mason helping. When the diner finally closed at three o'clock, Sophia thought she'd been through a war. If she couldn't sleep tonight she might as well shoot herself and call it quits.

She saw Pete and Mason talking in the kitchen.

"Sophia, I'll lock up you go on upstairs. You look like death warmed over."

"Thanks, Peter. Thanks a lot guys. I'll see you tomorrow. Mason, I'll see you when I see you." She waved tiredly and headed for her upstairs apartment. She was halfway up the stairs when she heard fast footsteps behind her.

"Wait up, honey."

"I'm sorry, I didn't think," she said not turning around. "You probably left some things up here. She trudged to the top floor and tried to open the door. It was locked. She turned to Mason.

"How did it get locked?"

"God, you're really out of it. You gave me the key hours ago so I could lock up. Don't you remember?"

Now she thought about it she vaguely remembered giving him her keys. He unlocked the door.

He ushered her inside and she slumped. He picked her up and put her down on the freshly made futon. She fell over sideways.

"Uh uh, no sleeping. Bath first, then bed." He left her, and she gave a tired laugh. Yeah sure she was going to sleep, like that was going to happen. She stared at the ceiling admiring the same damn crack. She heard the bath water running and then the cupboards opening. Eventually he came back.

"You didn't fall asleep," he said in a surprised voice. She turned her head to look at him. She gave a weak smile.

"What's sleep?"

"Fuck, that's not good."

He knelt beside the futon that served as her bed, and undressed her limp body. She was so tired it felt wonderful to be taken care of and naked. She knew she shouldn't feel like that. But she was too tired to fight it. He picked her up and took her into the small bathroom. He slid her gently into the bathtub and laid her head against a towel he'd rolled up. There was bath oil in the water. She'd forgotten she had that. God, the sensations were wonderful. Tears began to form. Then her eyes began to water. Oh God, please don't let her cry. He sat down beside the tub and looked at her.

"Wanna talk about it?" he asked as he picked up a cloth from the pile on the cabinet and handed it to her.

"No."

"Okay then, honey. Why don't you soak for a while? I'm going back downstairs and get the food Pete left for us. It'll be warm by the time you get out of the tub." She watched him leave. He was still in his white T-shirt and cargo shorts from the night before. What in the hell was he still doing here taking care of her, when he had just gotten home from God knows where? *Pull it together, Anderson.*

Sophia zoned out until she heard the door open and smelled the scent of pot roast. Then Mason was leaning on the frame of the bathroom door.

"Need help getting out of the tub?"

"No." Sophia pushed up with her arms but found they didn't work. She tried again and went down with a splash. She looked at him in surprise. She was in the process of getting up on her knees when he came up to her.

"Hey honey, I've got you. Your muscles are overworked. It's okay. I've been there." He gathered her into his arms and set her on the toilet seat.

"Mason, you're all wet."

"I'm a SEAL I like water." In seconds he had her wrapped in a towel, but she was shivering. "Hold on." He was back in just a blink with her favorite fleece sweats in his hands. He helped her into them just like she used to help Billy into his pajamas. He bent towards her.

"I can walk," she said quickly. He arched a brow, but she batted his hands away.

He still wrapped his arm around her waist, and they followed the heavenly scent of beef to the little table. He had two glasses of milk waiting. It was perfect. Within seconds she was shoveling, actually shoveling, food into her mouth. The last food she'd eaten was yesterday morning. *Damn crank calls.*

Mason was staring at her. Of course he was. She was eating like a prisoner who hadn't had a meal in five days.

"Sophia, you have to tell me what's been going on."

Oh no, now her stomach was beginning to cramp. She took a soothing drink of milk. Please settle, she begged her tummy.

"I'm just tired. You know about the nightmares. Then today Margie said she couldn't come in for a few days, so today was crazy. This is just all about me being tired."

"What about you not wanting my help?"

"I let you help me. Oh I'm sorry, I should have thanked you. God, I'm an ass. You were an absolute Godsend. Thank you so much."

"Jesus, that's not what I'm talking about baby. You would rather walk through burning coals than lean on me."

"That's not true." It was *so* true.

He looked at her. She couldn't meet his eyes. She looked at her food. She'd only finished half her plate. It felt like she'd eaten hers and Mason's plate. At least she didn't feel like throwing up anymore. Well she would if they kept talking about this.

"Can we not have this conversation now?" she begged. She could see the conflict on his face but he relented.

"Are you done?"

She nodded.

He took their plates into the kitchen area. He came back and helped her out of the chair, correctly guessing she needed the assistance.

"Let's get you into bed."

"Okay." She hoped the bath would help. She hadn't tried it before. He went into the bathroom and came back out holding a bottle of baby oil. He pulled off her fleece top and turned her onto her front.

"Honey, I want to try an experiment. Let's see if I can help you get some sleep, okay?"

She shivered as he brushed the hair over her shoulder onto the pillow. It was so cold but she also knew what was coming. She'd only had a handful of massages and never from a lover. She waited for him to squirt the oil on her back. She heard the bottle open and waited. Nothing. She peered up. He was warming it in his hand. Oh God, he made her heart swell. He trickled the warm oil down the center of her back and smoothed it into her skin in warm circles. He slowly moved upwards to her shoulders and started in on the tight muscles in her neck. She jerked in pain.

"Shhh, I know it hurts, honey."

She whimpered. He used his thumbs lightly at first and then as time went by increased the pressure.

"It's really hurting," she complained softly.

"Just a little bit more. I feel the knots. Let me get them out, okay?"

She nodded.

He pressed and prodded and she felt something give, and then for the first time in a week she felt like she could move her neck.

"Oh my God, what did you do?"

"Just relax. I'm not done yet." His magical hands kept going, down to the middle of her back, rubbing, and massaging. Sophia arched into the pressure, loving the feel. He used the heel of his hand on her lower back and she moaned. He swept upwards and then his fingers kneaded the muscles in her aching arms until finally their fingers were tangling and his head was close to hers. He kissed her temple.

Her body felt so light and airy. She felt him shift off the bed. Something warm touched her back. He was wiping off the oil with a washcloth.

"Okay love, now let's go to sleep. It's been a long day."

His warm naked body got in the bed behind hers and pulled her close. He was right. This time she could go to sleep. What a gift.

CHAPTER FOURTEEN

Mason knew the moment she came awake. She hadn't jerked in his arms, no cries, no whimpers, nothing like that for his girl, unless it was a nightmare. He waited a long while for her to try to get up or do something. She did nothing. As a matter of fact, she was working hard to keep her breathing even. She didn't want to disturb him. What was this need not to do anything to bother him? Why was she adamant not to come to him for support? He finally moved his arm and checked the glowing dial of his watch. Nine o'clock, she'd only slept for five hours, not nearly long enough.

"Sophia honey, what woke you?"

"Nothing." Now that was a line of bullshit if he ever heard one. He snuggled her closer.

"If nothing woke you up then let's go back to sleep. God knows I need to sleep until morning."

"Okay," came her soft reply. He waited and it took maybe ten minutes. The little minx changed her breathing to make it seem like she was asleep. Like he didn't know exactly what she sounded like sleeping. He'd memorized those sounds. He had soothed himself with them while in the jungle. Apparently it was time for their 'Come To Jesus' talk.

"Sophia, faking it won't work. I know what you sound like when you sleep. As a matter of fact, I know what you sound like when you come so don't try faking that either."

This time she jerked and giggled.

"I don't think there's any worry of that, Mr. Gault."

He turned on the bedside lamp and looked down at her.

"Oh, you plan to make sure I don't try to fake it, huh?" She smiled up at him.

He looked down at her beautiful face, so happy to see there were no traces of bruising. He kissed the jaw that had once been swollen and she sighed.

"We're going to have a little talk."

"But I thought…"

"Honey, why won't you ever let me help you?"

"Well you're already a team leader. You have enough people leaning on you the last thing you need is some wimpy ass female bugging the hell out of you. Don't worry, I promise not to be a burden. We're just having some fun. I understand that."

Just having fun? Was she out of her fucking mind? He'd been thinking about her night and fucking day. His mind refused to accept the words his ears just heard. He thought about to their time together, the look of joy on her face at the door last night. He wasn't wrong. This was more than a little bit of fun for her. Why had she said that?

"Is that what you want? Just some fun together? Because I want more."

"You can't," she said softly shaking her head.

"I do."

"Okay, then I can't. I can't risk it." Ah, now he finally heard truth.

"Can you explain it to me?"

"I've failed at every relationship I've ever had and you're becoming too important to me. If you walk away I don't think I could survive," she said on a choked sob. He tucked a strand of her hair behind her ear.

"I've seen how you are with Billy and Margie. You don't fail at relationships. You're their rock. You're fast becoming mine too."

"It's an act Mason. You haven't seen the real me." He couldn't comprehend what she was saying. He'd been with her during some of the most difficult times of her life, if that wasn't real he didn't know what was.

"You're not making any sense. Can you please explain it to me? Tell me about these relationships where you've failed. I want to understand."

"Okay, the truth is no matter how hard I try I end up being too needy. I might not be right now, but I will be and you'll hate me for it. I just know it." She turned away from him and looked out the small window. He turned her chin so she was forced to look at him.

"Sophia, you're the least needy person I know. As a matter of fact, you try to take on too much. I would love it if you would lean on me a little." She gave an inelegant snort.

"Yeah sure. A clingy female is what every man wants. Sign you up."

"Jesus, Sophia, you're not listening. Who the fuck did this number on you?"

"That's none of your business." She stiffened.

"It is too if it's keeping us from being together. I want you to explain yourself." He winced inwardly. He was even using his commander voice but nothing seemed to be getting through the walls Sophia built around herself.

"It's not one person it's two people. Well actually it's three if you count my dad."

"He sure as shit does count, if he made you feel this way."

Sophia couldn't help the wobble in her voice. "I was part of the reason dad left. He didn't leave mom on this last bout of cancer he left her the first time around when I was fifteen and Billy was five. He said he was tired of all the needy women in his life." Sophia remembered her dad looking her straight in the eye. It had been when her mom had been in the bathroom throwing up from the chemo treatments. He said she was a whiny, needy little girl and she should have grown up years ago. He was sick of her clinging to him and always wanting a pat on the back or a hug.

"Tell me," he begged.

"What?" Sophia looked at Mason. She had almost forgotten he was in the room with her.

"I want you to tell me exactly what just went through your head. Tell me the memory that has tears pouring down your face."

Sophia realized she was crying.

"I was fifteen and the washing machine broke. I only had my learner's permit so I couldn't drive to the laundromat. Dad was mad because he didn't have any clean clothes."

"I told him Mom was too sick to drive me and I asked for a ride." Sophia started to tremble. When Mason went to hold her she shook him away.

"Dad stormed into their bathroom and Mom was kneeling at the toilet throwing up because of the chemotherapy. He came back out, picked up the keys, drove me to the laundromat, and dropped me off."

"When I called for a ride home he was so angry because I hadn't dried the clothes and folded them. He said I didn't ever think. But I *had* thought. I didn't want to waste money. I knew our dryer at home was working. I thought he would be proud of me." Mason ached to hold her but she had her arms wrapped around herself and was rocking.

"He brought me home and I put some of the clothes in the dryer and went to help Mom. She was so sick and I started to cry. I'd forgotten we needed to go grocery shopping and there wasn't any of her favorite soup at home or any ginger ale." Mason knew he didn't want to hear what was coming next.

"I went to ask for a ride to the grocery store and he blew up. He yelled at me for crying, for being a whiny, sniveling little bitch just like my mom. He said I should have grown up years ago." Now she was sobbing.

"He walked out on us a week later."

"Motherfucker." He hauled her into his arms. She fought him, but he couldn't care less.

"I'm not done. When I was a junior in high school I had my first boyfriend. He said I was too clingy and I cramped his style. He dumped me and started dating a cheerleader the next week."

"Honey, he was a pimply faced little boy. That's what little high school boys do. You can't base your beliefs on that." Mason ran his hand down her back.

"But almost the exact same thing happened in college when I was a freshman. He was the only other man I ever slept with. His name was Lewis. He said I wanted too much from him. That I expected more than any man could ever possibly give." She shoved at his chest trying to get out of his arms but she was no match for his strength.

"You're going to finish it," he insisted.

"I found him in bed with another girl. He said he still loved me and we shouldn't break up. He said an adult woman would be able to get past it. That I was too needy. That my father was right about me."

Mason had to work hard to understand what she was saying because she was crying so hard but he knew he wanted to find the guy and pound him into dust.

"They were wrong, honey. They were all wrong. Each and every one of them should have realized the treasure you are."

She pushed at his chest again, but this time she reached out one hand to the night stand to pull out a wad of Kleenex.

"Yeah, some fucking treasure. Look at me, I'm crying all over you. I'm a mess." Again she tried to get out of his arms.

"Sophia, get it through your head I'm not letting go."

She looked up at him with dazed eyes.

"Just leave now before you break my heart."

He couldn't help his smile.

"If I could break your heart that means you've already given it to me. And I thank God, because girl, I've given you mine."

"You can't possibly mean it. I told you, I'll end up letting you down. I won't be enough for you." She looked so small and forlorn in his arms he had to gather her closer.

"Honey, you can't let me down. We're in this together. I've been falling in love with you since you told the doctor you'd been in a bar fight." She gave one of her giggle snorts he adored.

"You are so full of shit, Gault."

"Actually I'm not, honey. You showed so much bravery, such a good heart the way you cared about your brother and the young prostitute. I was so impressed by your intelligence and humor. There is a lot to like and admire about you."

"That's what I'm telling you—it's an act. I was just trying to keep it together that night. I was scared out of my mind and in so much pain." She gripped the front of his shirt to make her point, her voice pleading.

Mason could see he wasn't being heard. Sophia saw herself through the distorted mirror of those who had come before him. It was her father who really had the most to answer for. "Do you want me to go home? Is that what you want? Are you really going to make me leave tonight?" He was balancing on the thin edge of a sword. He was counting on the fact she wouldn't have the heart to make him leave. He watched as she struggled.

"No, you're just as tired as I am if not more so. Let's just get back to sleep."

Twenty minutes later they were right back to where they were before. Sophia was pretending to sleep. Mason knew how to solve the problem. It had worked that first night at his house and he'd be damned if he wasn't going try it again. Only there would be one change.

"You just tried to fake it again, Ms. Anderson." She let out a gasp as he pulled her hard against his chest and took one of her breasts in his warm hand, then gently trapped her head beneath his chin.

"Mason," his name another gasp, or was it a sigh?

"Right here, honey." He thumbed her nipple the way she liked and soon she was wiggling her butt against his cock just the way *he* liked. Back and forth, touching the tip that felt like a pebble encased in velvet. He moved his thumb up and put it to her lips.

"Suck my thumb, baby."

"Huh?"

"Suck it, get it nice and wet," he said as he brushed it against her lips. She finally took it into her mouth and his cock jerked painfully against her ass as she laved the digit with her tongue.

He jerked his thumb out of her mouth and went back to torturing her nipple, at least that's what he hoped he was doing, considering that's what was happening to him. Now he knew what she felt like, touching her like this was both the best and worst kind of torture in the world.

"Why are you doing this? We need to sleep."

Oh yeah, he was going to help her sleep. He pulled his hand away from her luscious tits and dragged it downwards, to forage beneath the soft fleece of her sweatpants. He knew she wasn't wearing underwear but finding her wet curls made him sweat. Everything about her was soft and silky, inviting and lush, and he savored her trust. She was panting and twisting.

"Mason, let me." She tried to roll over. He held her ruthlessly still. This was his show.

"In a few minutes, honey," he lied easily. That calmed her.

His fingers parted the seam of her sex and then she was no longer calm. She shuddered, so he knew he was doing something right. He moved his other hand and started playing with her neglected breast as two fingers thrust deep and started a bluesy rhythm.

"Mason," her voice sounded a musical counterpoint to his forays. Then he pressed down hard on her clit, and she screamed as she came.

Mason wasn't all that surprised by the huge sobs that came next. She'd dredged up a whole lot of shit to tell him tonight. Stuff that men, starting with that fucker of a father, had piled on top of her, and she still believed to be true.

"Let it out, honey," he crooned softly. He turned her around so her face was tucked under his chin. Then he wrapped his arms gently around her.

"One day when my nightmares get bad, and they do Sophia, I hope you'll hold me," he whispered. He felt her stop and look up at him through a cloud of tears.

"I know you don't believe me, but this is a two way street. We both lean on one another. You need to know something, honey. I wasn't completely honest earlier. I told you I was falling in love with you. Well I lied. I'm so far past falling. I am in deep, like quicksand deep, like ocean floor deep, and I've never been so happy. I love you, Sophia Anderson. Now why don't you lie here in my arms and not fall asleep, okay?"

"But Mason," she started.

"Uh unh, we're lying here pretending to be asleep, re-member?" He kissed the top of her head and started a slow rocking motion. She tried a couple of more times to talk, but each time he cut her off. Finally she started her fake sleeping routine. He checked his watch. It took exactly seven minutes for fake sleep to become real sleep. His took a hell of a lot longer. Maybe he would go find the asshole father in Mission Hills. He'd have to talk to his team. They'd either be with him, or explain why he was out of his mind. His team always had his back. With that thought he finally slept as well.

CHAPTER FIFTEEN

It'd been four or five days since her attempt at breaking up, and Sophia had never been happier. It was Saturday afternoon and she was going to close up the diner, get ready to go over to Mason's house, and spend all of Sunday with him. She had a big surprise ready for him and his teammates.

"Brenda, I'm so glad you were able to come to work on a full time basis," Sophia said to the woman who was in her early thirties.

"Yeah, well it's been different but okay I guess. Thanks for the paycheck." She shoved it into her oversized purse and walked out the front.

It was terrible but Sophia didn't like her. Not once had she asked how Margie or her daughter-in-law were doing. She just did the bare minimum to get by. She only really smiled when she thought it would help get her a tip. She needed to talk to Margie, it was time they started looking for someone new and then fire Brenda. What's more, there was the ugly shit with Tate, Brenda's boyfriend. Sophia grimaced. But she firmly put that crap behind her. She'd handled it. She locked the front door of the diner, turned around, and grinned.

She walked through the empty diner towards the back staircase to her apartment, thinking through her plans. She really hadn't wanted Margie to come down to San Diego, but when she'd talked to her, Margie sounded like she could use a break. Helen's mom was going to come over and watch the kids and Margie was going to spend tonight in La Jolla with a friend. She and her friend would be over at Mason's Sunday afternoon with enough food to feed an Army or a Navy, she quickly corrected herself.

Frannie and Tony would be over two hours before the festivities began. They had a lot of questions about Mason's kitchen, so Sophia knew she had to get her baking done early while Mason and Billy were gone. She still couldn't believe Mason had taken it upon himself to call the Bards and request to take Billy surfing. Talk about being ocean deep in love, Sophia planned to tell him tonight that she loved him too.

Sophia looked at her phone to check the time and realized she better get a move on. She flew up the stairs and was showered, dressed, packed, and out the door in less than an hour. She could have been done sooner but a gal had to put some time in front of the mirror to look good for her guy. Especially when he was the handsomest man on the face of the planet. Yeah, get a towel and wipe the drool off your chin girl, she said as she headed for her car.

Her phone rang. "Sheesh, I'm on my way already."

"On your way where?" She dropped her phone. She looked at the asphalt and stared at the pretty pink rubber wrapped case in horror. She wanted to stomp on her phone.

Cool it, Anderson, no replacements phones for conniption fits.

She waited two more minutes. Picked it up and hurriedly pressed end before anyone could speak. It creeped her out that there had still been someone on the phone. She checked history. Yep, still an unknown caller. *Great.*

She was trembling when she got behind the wheel of the car. She took some deep breaths and thought through her crank call issue.

She'd actually gone through her call history yesterday. In the last three weeks, she'd had fifteen hang-ups from unidentified callers. Some during the day but most in the middle of the night. She needed to talk to Mason about this. He was going to be pissed if she didn't *share*. The problem was she really thought it was Brenda's boyfriend. The calls started after her confrontation with him. Sophia winced. That was another thing she was going to have to *share*. Occasionally she considered that it was one of her attackers, but that was just to awful to bear, so she focused on Tate.

Now she had her sharing plan figured out, she could concentrate on the great surprise she'd planned for Mason and his team. The drive down to San Diego was beautiful. It was one of those clear days when you rolled the windows down, breathed in the ocean, and felt like the blue of the Pacific could suck you in with its beauty. *How lucky am I to be able to drive on a freeway with this kind of scenery? Okay, I might be a little over the top just to compensate for the call, but hey, whatever it took, right?*

By the time Sophia got to Mason's house all thoughts of the call were gone, and when he opened the door she was grinning. He scooped her up and she squealed with delight.

"I missed you. It felt weird to sleep in my bed without you last night."

"But you did sleep some, right?" He asked with concern. He set her down and cupped her cheeks tracing the hollows under her eyes.

"Some, I slept a little bit." She refused to lie anymore. He kissed the tip of her nose for her honest answer. He drew her into the kitchen and poured her a glass of lemonade. She took two long sips.

"Well, you'll sleep tonight and tomorrow we'll have a hell of a barbeque. I can't believe you're willing to go to

Costco with me. All of those people and lines give me the heebie-jeebies."

"Come on, you must love all the free samples," she teased him. She saw the lines at the corner of his eyes fan out.

"You caught me. It's the one thing that makes it bearable and most of those ladies remind me of my nana. You're going to love meeting her." She pulled back and stared at him. He just cocked an eyebrow.

"Deal with it, Anderson. I don't want any guff from you. You're going to have to deal with the hell of knowing you're the type of girl I want to take home to meet my family."

A load of sawdust landed in her mouth and throat. Luckily it was hard packed, so she didn't cough, but she needed more lemonade.

"Come on, my family isn't scary. They're nice. You'll like them, I swear." She gave him an incredulous look.

"Of course I'll like them, you doofus. The question is what will they think of me?" He was out of his mind it was just that simple. "So when are they coming to visit?"

"They aren't. I was thinking the two of us could take a trip up north in a few months to see them. It'll be great. Maybe around Thanksgiving? You should have custody of Billy by then so he should be able to come too, right?"

"Boy, when you decide to go all in you really do it, don't you?" His eyes were steady. She set down the glass and pulled him off of his barstool and dragged him into the living room.

"Why are we in here?"

"I want to sit on your lap."

His eyes warmed and he pulled her down, then she situated herself perfectly so she was cuddled close.

"So you've decided to cement our relationship with family holiday trips even though I haven't committed to you, huh?"

"Yep. I've decided to wear you down."

"I don't like that method." Sophia bit his chin sharply. "The man I love shouldn't sell himself that cheaply. He should expect his woman to throw rose petals at his feet because he's the best man in the world, and she loves him soul deep." Sophia stared into eyes bluer than the Pacific Ocean and saw all of her hopes and dreams coming true.

* * *

Everything stilled. He was going to remember this moment for the rest of his life. He captured her lips. She tasted different, softer, more open, as if she was finally letting him in. He cherished her gift. He continued to explore the texture of her mouth, lost in the feel of her molding to his body. He could stay like this forever, until he couldn't. He had to get her to his bedroom or explode in the living room. Mason stroked her back up and down, loving how she arched into his touch, and he finally eased her away. She whimpered.

"We're going down the hall."

"Oh." She looked at him with glazed eyes. "The bedroom's good."

He put one arm around her back and one under her knees.

"I love it when you carry me," she whispered. He'd wondered. It was something that had made him feel satisfied, but she'd seemed reluctant yet somewhat content. He hadn't been sure. Again, he was glad he had followed his instincts. He soon had her lying on his bed. He looked at her and admired her honey gold hair spilled out against his navy blue comforter. It looked gold, and silver, and red with the afternoon sun streaming in through the window.

Mason ached. He needed her so badly. He always did. All he had to do was think of Sophia Anderson and his body went into overdrive, but today was different. Today was the start of something.

Now she finally admitted to loving him, they were going to have a future together. Mason had known for a while now Sophia was the one. He wanted to marry this woman, build a life with her, grow old with her, and when the day came, he wanted to die in her arms. Knowing that, he intended to have this joining be a memorable foundation that would start their lives together.

* * *

Hours later Mason's body was still thrumming with the satisfaction of having loved Sophia.

"I'm going to try this leaning thing. Do you mind if I work my way up to it?"

Mason felt some of the knots in his shoulders loosen. He thought he was going to have to get the crowbar out of his trunk to get her to talk.

"Do you think you can let me know what the problem is tonight?" Mason asked hopefully. He looked over at Sophia as they sipped their milkshakes. They were at the beach, having just grabbed their drinks at the shack near the ocean. It turned out they both loved the place. Sophia was staring off into the ocean and he was mostly staring at her. She was absolutely gorgeous with the sunset glinting off her skin. But, he also knew underneath the pink tint she was pale from lack of sleep.

"Yes," she said as she continued to look out over the water. Mason's shoulders relaxed even more.

The first couple of days after Margie left to help her daughter-in-law had been rough. Once again Sophia did it all. He'd never been so thankful to see such a skank as Brenda show up. The woman had made three heavy handed passes at him, even though it was obvious he and Sophia were a couple. He hated women like Brenda. What's more, she did the least amount of work possible, and left all the heavy lifting to Sophia. Yep, Brenda was a real winner but at least she took some of the stress off of his girl.

Still the extra burden at the diner didn't explain everything. He knew she was still having nightmares when they weren't sleeping together. He was going to talk to her about seeing a counselor again. Dammit, it seemed like he was busy pushing her on a lot of different fronts, but she didn't have many people who were there for her. Margie was so busy with her own family, and the DeLucas weren't around all that much. Basically Sophia was on her own, and Mason knew it brought out his protective instincts.

She turned to him as she sucked down the last of her milkshake and gave him a woeful glance.

"What?" He gave her an unbelieving look.

"Mine's empty."

"It's not my fault you have no self-control." He suppressed a grin.

"I'm still thirsty." Her expression went from woeful to pitiful.

"Did this ever work?"

"It does every time Billy does it to me." She gave him the cutest grin ever.

"Come here." She looked at him quizzically. He reached over and arranged for her to be sitting between his spread legs, and resting against his chest.

"This is nice."

He put the straw against her lips and she took a small sip. He brought it back to his mouth, and could swear he could taste Sophia along with the chocolate, and it made the treat all the better. They continued in silence, watching the setting sun and enjoying the rest of the drink. When it was dark he had a sleeping Sophia in his arms. He hated to wake her but it was chilly.

"Come on, honey, time to go home."

"I love waking up in your arms."

Now didn't that make him feel like a million dollars? They made their way up the beach to his parked truck. Her phone rang on the way. She tensed up and pulled it out of her hoodie to look at the display. Then she pressed ignore.

"That's part of what we have to talk about, but that's the last part, okay?"

"Sure honey, just tell me things at your own pace."

He opened the passenger door for her, and once again she seemed surprised even though he'd done it every time they got into his truck.

They talked about his house remodel, Pete, Margie, and her daughter-in-law, but when he asked how she was feeling about the upcoming court case she clammed up.

"Have you talked to the D.A. at all, honey? I thought Mrs. Porter said she would stay in touch."

"Yeah, she called me. She said they set a court date for the end of July." Sophia sounded like she was chewing on glass. He grabbed her hand. It was a tightly clenched fist. He quickly looked over at her. He could see the outline of her face against the passenger window and her jaw was rigid.

"She brought me in for a debriefing or something while you were gone. It was horrible. She pretended she was their lawyer. She made it sound like I was a prostitute who liked it rough and that I actually agreed to have sex with them for money. Otherwise why was I there so late at night?"

Mason looked ahead for the next exit and took it.

Within five minutes he had them parked in a Denny's parking lot. He lifted up the console and slid over, and then arranged for her to be straddling his lap. She gripped his shirt. She didn't cry. She made no noise at all. She just rested her head against his chest in defeat.

"You know Mrs. Porter was doing that to practice with you."

"Sure, I've watched enough TV. But I also know at the end of July I'm going to have to be on the witness stand and somebody is going to say those ugly things about me in front of twelve jurors. What's more, those same men and women are going to see pictures of me."

Huge shudders went through her body. Then he understood. The bruising on her torso, and on her breasts.

"Ah fuck." He rocked her back and forth but still she didn't shed a tear. It was as if the pain went too deep for mere tears. "It's going to be all right, I promise you. There is no way anyone will believe what those bastards are saying."

"I keep spinning around in circles. I can't seem to stop my mind just chewing and chewing on this. Sometimes I want to scream that I was the one who was abused, and I shouldn't have to be put through this," her voice was a whisper into his sweatshirt. Then her head came up and she looked him in the eye.

"Then there are other times I want to grind them into little pieces of dust. I want to get up there and have them do their worst. Show those pictures so they can see them for the animals they are. It doesn't matter if I was a prostitute, they assaulted me. They were going to rape me. The one man..." She stopped.

"What honey, tell me."

She pushed her face into his chest and shook her head.

"If you won't tell me then tell a professional. These dreams you've been having are debilitating. You're not getting nearly enough sleep. I worry about you so much."

"I don't want to see anyone," her tone vehement.

"Then can you tell me?"

She was quiet for so long he thought she would never answer. He held her and watched as cars came in and left the restaurant parking lot.

"If you hadn't come the one man would have killed me after he raped me. I know it…" her voice trailed off.

"I believe you, honey."

"You do?"

"I do. You've got to remember what I do for a living. I've looked into the eyes of evil before. I know what it's like to stare at someone who wants you dead."

She gripped the front of his shirt, her nails biting into his chest.

"That's it, that's it exactly. He wanted me dead. It excited him. That's what got him off—the idea of killing me. The other man wanted to violate me, but the first man, he wanted to kill me." She started to cry. Mason could only pray now she had said the words, got them out in the open, her nightmares would begin to dissipate. He gathered her close and murmured words he prayed would bring her comfort. All the while his mind was whirling with the fact this bastard was currently out on bail.

"Oh, God I'm…"

He tilted up her chin she was forced to meet his eyes.

"If the next word out of your mouth is going to be sorry, I'm going to be pissed. You have nothing to be sorry about. You're not being needy. This would bring anyone to their knees. But even if you were being clingy, I would love it because I *love* you."

"I'm holding you to that because I'm not done."

"Okay, I'm listening."

"I've been getting these calls, they were just hang ups, and then yesterday they talked to me."

"Jesus, why didn't you tell me before this?" Mason winced at the tone of his voice, especially when Sophia drew back.

"Honey, I'm sorry."

"No, you're right. I should have told you. I didn't think about it. It was a nuisance, and then when it really started to escalate you were gone," she said, her voice trembling. Mason pulled her back into his arms.

"Shhh, the important thing is you told me now. How many calls do you think you've gotten? Did it start after the D.A. gave your contact information to the asshole's attorney?"

"I don't think it's them, it started after I had a run in with Brenda's boyfriend."

"What kind of run in?"

"He and Brenda were having some problems. He made a couple of pretty strong passes." How had he missed this?

"How long has that been going on?"

"It started almost exactly the day you started coming to the diner. It was weird." Mason snorted.

"Honey, it's not weird. He probably always had a thing for you, but it wasn't until some other man was showing some interest that he knew he needed to make his move. You should have told me immediately. What do you mean by a strong pass?" Sophia blew out a deep breath.

"One time he trapped me near the bathroom and kissed me, another time he caught me outside and grabbed my breast. I kneed him in the balls. Since then he's kept his hands to himself."

"And you worry about being clingy. It just boggles the mind." Mason pulled out his phone and pressed his speed dial for Clint, who answered on the second ring.

"Can you come over to my house? It's important." Sophia looked at him like he had grown a second head. "Thanks, man."

He kissed the tip of Sophia's nose. "Come on, let's get you buckled we've got to get home."

* * *

Clint was waiting for them on the porch when they pulled up. He followed them into the house and Mason pulled out a beer for him. Clint set a small computer tablet on the kitchen island.

"Sophia, can you give him your phone." Sophia rifled through her purse. The whole thing seemed bizarre but she trusted Mason. Both men looked serious.

"So what's the deal?" Clint asked Mason.

"She's been getting a lot of hang-ups."

"Shit."

"Here." She handed her phone to Mason.

"Honey, I need you to unlock it first." Damn, of course he did. She took it back and entered her password. She couldn't see what he was doing but she assumed from his grim expression he was scrolling through her recent calls.

"There have been fifteen times where I actually answered and someone hung up. Then there are the times when I just let it ring."

"Sophia, somebody has been calling you at least three times a day. Sometimes at two o'clock or four o'clock in the morning." He handed back her phone and turned to his computer.

"I know, that's why I told Mason." She saw both men's jaws clench. The only saving grace was Drake wasn't there.

"Sophia, what's your number?"

She gave it to him.

"Any suspects?" he asked Mason.

"All of San Diego."

"Doesn't he need my phone?"

"Nope, I just needed your phone number." Clint's fingers started flying over the keyboard.

"What are you going to do?" Sophia asked. Clint didn't answer.

"What would you like to drink?" Mason asked her. "Clint won't answer, he won't even talk for a while. He's in the zone."

Sophia peered at the tablet and saw a bunch of code.

"Are you sure he'll be able to help."

"Oh, he'll find out who's been calling you."

"I don't understand. How could he possibly do that?"

"That's what we do. We figure shit out. If one of us can't do it, trust me, the other one knows how to get it done."

Sophia pulled flour and sugar out of the pantry and then got the butter out of the fridge.

"What are you doing?" Mason asked.

"It's what I do. I bake."

Clint looked up from the computer. "Cherry pie?" he asked hopefully.

Two pies later Clint had answers for Sophia, which left her scared and confused. Then Mason took her into his arms and she knew it was going to be okay.

CHAPTER SIXTEEN

Mason was exhilarated. It was a perfect day. The sun was warm on his face. He'd worked up a head of steam playing with Billy. Now the boy was on the beach with Sophia, Mason could really cut loose. He pulled himself through the ocean on his board, paddling even harder feeling the burn in his shoulders and chest. Out of the corner of his eye he could see a large swell coming towards him. He jumped up the board, balanced, and everything receded. Just this one moment in time existed as he concentrated and grinned like a madman.

He balanced and flew, the water on his face felt glorious, the warm sky, the smell of the ocean and the cry of the gulls all coalesced together to make a perfect moment. He was in the tube, and it seemed to last forever. Even the crash into the water made him happy, today was nothing but joy.

Mason continued on for another hour before hunger had him heading for the beach, eager to see what Sophia had packed for a mid-morning snack. Then he started at a faster pace realizing he shouldn't have left a hungry pre-teen boy with the food as long as he had.

"Oh my God, you should see your face." Sophia laughed. He was thrilled with how carefree she sounded. It hit him, she was only twenty-two and she didn't act like someone that young.

"Mason?"

"Huh?"

"Now you're staring at me. Before you were staring at the picnic basket with the most woeful expression. What is going on with you?"

"Must be the sun." He dismissed her concern. "Did Billy leave any food for me?" he asked, staring at the blond boy lounging next to his sister eating what looked like homemade strudel.

"Are you kidding, Mase? Soph made enough for an army." Then Billy sat up and peered into the basket. "Well maybe not an army." He reached in, and Sophia slapped his hand.

"You've had more than enough. I've seen you get carsick and I don't want you throwing up in Mason's truck."

"That's when I was a little kid," Billy protested.

"Hell Billy, what's a little puke between friends. But if you eat one more bite of this food I'm going to have to beat you." Mason sat and put the basket between his legs, sorting through the contents. He found a bottle of water and he used it to wash down the breakfast burrito.

"God, this is wonderful Sophia. It is better than my favorite food truck near the base." He loved it when she blushed.

"You eat at food trucks? That's so cool." Billy tried to reach towards the basket, and this time Mason slapped him away. Billy just grinned.

Mason grabbed a huge breakfast sandwich that had thick slices of grilled ham. He thought he'd gone to heaven. When the hell had Sophia had time to make this? They'd gotten up at the ass crack of dawn. This he ate a little more slowly and washed down with a bottle of orange juice.

"Wow, you're fast. It took me almost a half hour, and you ate those in like five minutes."

Now he felt his cheeks heat. He'd obviously been out on missions too damn often, when he needed to wolf down his food and be on his way. But he sure as hell wasn't going to tell either of the Anderson siblings that.

"I guess I was hungry, plus you were eyeing the food too closely, Billy. I knew I had to eat or lose my chance." Billy snickered. Sophia looked at him curiously. That woman was too smart for her own damn good. It was ten o'clock by the time they were making their way back to the house. His team was due to arrive at two.

* * *

Sophia's plan was working perfectly. By the time Billy and Mason got out of their showers it was eleven.

"I want to get a couple of things baked for the horde before they get here. Can you and Billy do the Costco run without me?"

"Sure honey, but you owe me for bailing." He came over and ran his hand over her hair and kissed her. "Guess you finally get to sit in the front seat Billy," he teased.

"I'll be right there, Mase."

Mason gave Sophia a quizzical look, but headed out the door.

"What's up, Billy?"

"How serious are you and Mase?"

Shit, she hadn't been expecting that question.

"We're dating."

"Are you going to get married?"

Yep, hadn't considered this at all.

"Billy, we've only been together for a little over a month. I can't imagine Mason wanting to marry me." She watched as Billy worked to digest her answer. He went over to the fridge and pulled out a sports drink. He put it on the island and fiddled with the cap.

"Soph, I don't want you to be sad, okay? I know you're having sex. So if you guys aren't getting married you'll break up, and you'll be sad. I don't want you hurt." He abandoned the drink and came over to her and gave her a hug. It was then she realized he came up to her chin. When had he gotten so tall? So smart?

She kissed the top of her baby brother's head and tipped his chin so she could look him in the eye.

"Mason and I love each other. I'm not sure where we'll end up." Sophia's gut clenched. She couldn't imagine a time without him in her life.

"I hope you get married. He's a really good guy, Soph, you deserve someone really good." He looked away and grabbed his drink and was out the door before she could say another word.

"Billy Anderson, I just met another really good guy today," she murmured. She pulled out all of the ingredients she was going to need to feed the army of people who would be coming over. She didn't have much time, since the DeLucas would soon be commandeering the stove and oven. She called Drake yesterday and let him know the time for the party was going to be two-thirty. Billy knew to stall Mason at the store so he came home at the same time. All of Sophia's 'food winnings' should be here and ready by two o'clock. She had a cake and brownies cooling by the time the DeLucas arrived with their food.

"Sophia, can you help us unload the car?" Frannie asked.

"No problem." When Sophia went to their station wagon she was amazed. There were four large pans for the oven, and five sauce pans. Then there were covered glass containers with tin foil. The entire back of the station wagon was packed full with food. She stood there.

"We're Italian," Tony said proudly. He handed her a warm pan and motioned her towards the house. Soon Margie's ride pulled up in a Mercedes. Sophia wondered if her friend might be a boyfriend. She had her answer, he was. He was about Margie's age and he immediately saw the dilemma and laughed. He started to pitch in, helping to clear out the station wagon, while introducing himself at the same time.

"I'm Mel," he said to Sophia as he handed her another pan. "I belong to Margie." Sophia was delighted with the way Margie blushed. He then handed Margie a light pan containing garlic bread.

"Here sweetie, you take this inside and then rest up. I'll take care of everything else. You've been cooking up a storm."

"I can help."

"Now Margie, please let me do this for you."

Margie opened her mouth to protest, but he planted a kiss on her lips stifling what she was going to say. By the time he was done she was looking a little dazed.

"All right Mel, but don't think you can win every argument this way."

"I wouldn't dream of it, sweetie. But seriously, you deserve a break." *Oh my.*

They walked into the kitchen and deposited their pans of food, and found the DeLucas hard at work.

"I love this kitchen, Sophia. Your young man has done a great job on his renovation," Frannie praised.

"Where are we going to eat? The dining room isn't finished," Tony asked.

"We'll be eating out back. He has a huge picnic table and I asked Drake to bring an extra table and chairs."

"So you have a co-conspirator." Margie winked. "I like that boy."

"I hope not too much," Mel said, as he patted a stool for Margie to sit down.

"I was going to help Frannie and Tony."

"You're going to sit and visit. Sophia and I will bring in the rest of the food and get to know one another."

"Margie, you can ice the cakes now that they've cooled." Mel gave Sophia a winning smile. It took them four more trips to bring in everything from the DeLuca's car and Mel's Mercedes. There were pitchers of lemonade and sangria waiting for them by the time they were done.

"I'll take lemonade for now," Sophia said when Tony offered her a choice. She checked the clock over the stove and realized Drake would be over soon. He knew she'd invited some of her friends over, but he didn't realize she'd arranged for the SEAL team to be fed. He thought it was the normal barbeque and beer.

Just then she heard Drake's souped-up truck pull up into the carport. She rushed outside, not wanting him to see all the activity in the kitchen.

"Hey gorgeous, I brought some hired help to move this mother." She giggled at the mound of table and chairs tied down in the back of the truck. There was no way she would have been able to figure out how to have fit everything, but it was all tied down neat and orderly. When she said as much, Drake grinned.

"Hell, they teach this damn the near the first day in the Navy. You can't have things falling off the ship." Clint was already carrying three chairs to the backyard.

"So what kind of surprise do you have planned for us? Does it have anything to do with the heavenly scents coming from the kitchen?" Drake asked.

"You're just the hired help today. You get the table set up and I'll bring out a couple of appetizers and some beer."

"That sounds good to me. We did some physical training and I'm starved," Clint said as he grabbed the last of the chairs. When she went back into the kitchen she found a plate of antipasto, and bruschetta waiting.

"Here's the tablecloths, Sophia," Frannie said as she handed them over.

"I need to get a couple of beers." Sophia opened the refrigerator.

"Take the sangria and lemonade. We also brought some nice wines. The boys can have beer of course. But let them know that they have other options."

"Beer will go great with my brisket," Margie chimed in.

"She's right about that," Mel agreed.

Sophia grabbed the beers, took the table cloths, and made her escape while her friends argued the merits of different foods and beverages.

"Tablecloths? Just what are you feeding us?" Drake asked.

"Just shut up and help the woman. I get the feeling we're in for a treat," Clint said as he set the two beers down on the grass and helped Sophia spread out the material on the tables. She turned around as she heard two cars and a truck show up.

"Looks like everyone is on time. Do we get our food now?" Drake asked with a hopeful look.

"I fooled him!" Billy said as he bounded up towards Sophia. She looked at her brother who was once again acting like the boy she was used to. She looked up at Mason who was approaching at a slower pace. He was looking around with a warm smile.

"It looks like you've been busy."

"I won at poker while you were away. Today I'm collecting my winnings." The other men walked up and said hello.

"Hi guys, why don't you have a seat and enjoy the appetizers. We'll bring out the food and drinks. You don't have to do a thing."

"Oh hell no," Drake said. "We're going to help."

"'You'll do as the lady says," Tony DeLuca said as he carried a huge pan of eggplant parmigiana to the table. "My name is Tony, and it is our honor to serve you. But all bets are off once the food hits the table."

Frannie, Margie and Mel came next with more food. All of the men stood up as the ladies brought out plates of food. Tony introduced them. Then Mason introduced his SEAL team.

"I want to know more about this poker game Sophia said she won," Mason asked.

"Never saw anything like it. Turns out Sophia doesn't know how to bluff. She only bet when she had the cards to back herself up. By the time we all figured it out she had won."

"So how is it we ended up with this great food?" Darius wanted to know.

"We play for food. Whoever loses has to make the other one dinner. Usually I win so Margie and Frannie make me their specialties. Because Sophia won, we all owed her a dinner. It was her idea to come down here and cook for all of you."

Everyone was looking at her and she hated it. Mason realized it and took her hand underneath the table and gave it a reassuring squeeze. Some of the tension eased.

"Must have been beginner's luck," Finn said as he took a bite of brisket. He wiped his mouth and stared over at Margie. "Ma'am, this is to die for. I used to go to my grandmother's house in Texas and she would serve brisket every Sunday, but it was nothing compared to this. Are you from Texas?"

"No, but my Mama was. She taught me. It's all a matter of seasoning and slow cooking this on a low enough temperature so the meat falls off the bone. Now try some of my cornbread." Sophia watched as each man gravitated to a different type of food, which pleased each of the cooks.

"Your team is nice."

"They're not being nice, they're being real. This is amazing. Only you would think to do something like this. Billy never gave anything away either, I'm amazed."

Sophia warmed under his praise. She looked around and saw how Margie and Mel were seated at one table with some of Mason's friends, and the DeLuca's were over here with Mason and the rest of the team. She loved that everybody was mingling.

"Can I get you something to drink or do you just want more lemonade?"

"Have some Chianti," Tony suggested as he poured a glass. "Here, it helps with digestion. You've hardly eaten anything." He turned to Mason. "You need to watch her, when she gets nervous she doesn't eat."

Frannie pulled Sophia's plate and gestured to all of the dishes around the table. "What do you want sweetie, because you're going to eat something." Sophia knew she was out gunned. Only Darius and Tony had come back for seconds of Frannie's Hungarian goulash, so it was an easy choice.

"You're right Frannie, I did get nervous, but I've been really wanting more goulash and sour cream and some of your homemade bread." Frannie beamed. She got a bowl and dished out a huge helping that Sophia wouldn't be able to eat even if she had gone without food for three days.

"Save room for Tony's cannoli," Frannie warned her.

"I will."

"I can't believe you organized all of this, honey," Mason whispered in her ear. Sophia looked at him.

"What makes you think I couldn't organize something like this?" She'd been taking care of her mom for over two years. She was more than capable of throwing together a party.

"Honey, I'm not talking about putting it together and the surprise part. I'm talking about how much this really means to me and the guys. Having Tony, Margie and Frannie cook us a home cooked meal means a lot."

Sophia looked around the tables and saw the pleasure on the other men's faces and saw Mason was right. It was what she'd hoped for. What's more, she could see the contentment the older people were exuding at having contributed.

"Mason, as long as you and I are dating let's continue to do this," she said with an excited smile.

Mason gave her a long look, and then finally nodded.

"I agree, this should become a tradition for us," he said as he put his arm around her shoulder.

* * *

Mason realized she hadn't even heard what she had said. As far as Sophia was concerned there was going to come a time when they wouldn't be together. She was positive he would abandon her much like her father left her mother. Mason was having a hard time figuring out how to convince her otherwise. He sure as hell didn't want to be on his twenty-fifth wedding anniversary with his wife still wondering when he was going to leave.

Sophia was taking small bites of her goulash, determined to eat as much as she could to please Frannie.

"Honey, you're not going to hog all of that, are you?" Mason said as he picked up his spoon. He took a big bite of the succulent dish, and immediately went in for more. Soon his and Sophia's spoons were clicking as they both fought over the drops at the bottom of the bowl.

Sophia then picked up a piece of homemade bread, broke off half, swiped up some of the soup and held it out to Mason's lips.

"Here, try this."

He took the offered bite, making sure to taste the tips of her fingers.

"It's delicious." He loved watching the blush bloom under her golden skin. It made her freckles stand out even more and made her even more beautiful. Sophia glanced across the table to see if anyone was looking at them, but he didn't care, he continued to keep his eyes on her.

"I have to go get the desserts," she whispered.

"I'll help."

"Don't help too much. We want the desserts to eventually arrive," Drake teased good-naturedly. Sophia's blush turned neon as she scurried into the house. Mason just shook his head, realizing she was going to have to get used to being around his friends.

"You shouldn't do that to her, Drake," he heard Margie chiding his friend as he followed Sophia into the door.

Sophia was pulling out a tray of cannoli from the fridge. He took it from her and put it on the counter.

"Look, chocolate cream. I know you always order it at the diner."

"Hmmm. You're taking care of me again."

"It's becoming one of my favorite things in the world to do."

Why the fuck were there so many people at his house? He needed Sophia. Shoving his fingers into the silk of her hair, he positioned her head and swooped in for a kiss. She opened up, and he was lost in the warmth, taste, and texture of Sophia. His thumbs traced her cheekbones and he was once again awed at the soft feel of her skin. She slid her tongue against his and pressed her body closer.

His heart was beating so loud he thought he must be having a heart attack.

"Mase, desserts? Remember?" Drake. How could he have been so caught up in Sophia he hadn't realized Drake was pounding on the kitchen door? He brushed back Sophia's hair and gave her one last kiss.

"No," she protested as he broke away.

"Drake's here, honey," he whispered against her temple.

"Don't care." He stared into her passion glazed eyes and swept in for another kiss. He didn't care either. She slid her tongue along his bottom lip, and then thrust inside his mouth. He felt claimed by the small dynamo in his arms. She pushed her breasts hard against his chest and then grabbed his hand and pulled it away from her waist and up to her chest.

"You have company here in the kitchen…" Fuck. He cupped her cheeks and pulled away so that he could rest his forehead on hers.

"Tonight, honey. We'll get rid of the riffraff tonight."

"I resemble that comment," Drake said as he bit into a cannoli.

Sophie turned in his arms and stared at Drake. "Those are for everyone. How many have you had?"

"You were kissing for a long time. You were in front of the silverware drawer, and I couldn't cut into the pies so I had to make due."

"Dammit Drake, after all the food you guys just consumed you're going to eat this much dessert too?" Mason grinned. She sure had come a long way in her dealings with Drake since they'd first met.

"Only if everything tastes this good," Drake said reaching for another treat. Sophia sped over to him and slapped his hand.

"You've had more than enough. Take the tray out to the others. Mason, you take the pies. I've got to rustle up a few more things."

Mason watched as she looked around the kitchen. He waited until Drake left and then looked at her.

"Sophia, this will be more than enough. You don't need to stress about anything."

"I'm not stressed. I made a few other things for Billy to take home to the Bards, and for you to have next week while I'm working at the diner." He watched as she opened the breadbox and pulled out a stash of cookies and then went to the pantry and pulled out the rest of the strudel. He wondered if there had been more. He waited, hoping. She then pulled out a tin of brownies. Score!

"I see that look. That was supposed to be the big surprise."

"Pecans?"

"Yes, they have pecans."

"Please put them back in the pantry, I'm begging you," Mason said as he snagged two of the treats out of the tin.

"Nope, they are going to the hungry horde out in the yard."

He loved it when she got that bossy, pissy voice. It was such a turn on.

The kitchen door opened. "Since you're not kissing what's taking the food so long?"

"Carry this, asshole." Mason shoved the two pies at Drake, but made sure to keep the tin of brownies in one of his hands as he carried the strudel in the other. Sophia followed with the cookies. Boy did this woman know how to spoil the people she cared about.

CHAPTER SEVENTEEN

The party couldn't have been more of a success. The seniors and the SEALs were thrilled and they all seemed to think it was her doing. But she had done very little. Before her face turned permanently red from the compliments, she took the opportunity to drive Billy home.

"I can do it," Drake offered.

"No, I want to spend as much time as possible with him," Sophia said with all sincerity. Drake smiled and nodded.

"We'll do it together," Mason said, giving her hand a squeeze as she stood to wave Billy over to her. "Drake, can you handle clean-up?"

"Yep."

Mason, Sophia, and Billy said their thanks and goodbyes to everyone. Billy was on cloud nine. He talked about surfing and the great dinner all during the drive back to his foster parents.

"When can we go surfing again?" Billy asked.

"How about next weekend. As long as I'm in town that should work."

"That would be great! Don't worry, Soph, I've been mowing yards. I've saved up enough money to rent my wetsuit this next time." God, she loved her little brother.

"That's great, but why don't you keep your money? I've got it covered. Margie gave me a raise since I'm now supervising employees."

"That's awesome but I'm still paying," Billy insisted.

Sophia opened her mouth to disagree again but Mason reached over and squeezed her thigh. She looked up and he gave a quick shake of his head. She thought it over and realized he was right. It would be good for Billy to take responsibility.

"Thanks, I really appreciate you chipping in."

Billy beamed.

By the time they dropped him off he'd wound down a little, and Sophia hoped he could sleep.

When they got back to Mason's house everyone was gone, and there was no sign a party had ever taken place.

"What the hell? How is this even possible?" Sophia said as she looked around the kitchen.

"You put a Navy man in charge things get done," Mason said. "Do you know how great today was? I haven't seen the team this happy in ages. It was especially meaningful to Finn."

"Why?"

"He's really missing his grandfather, and I could see him soaking up the time with Tony."

Now Mason mentioned it, Sophia had noticed Finn and Tony talking a lot.

"You Sophia Anderson are one special lady." Where the praise had been embarrassing earlier from the others, from Mason it just warmed her.

"I was pretty sure it would be a success but part of me was nervous. I didn't want to screw up in front of your friends."

"My friends love you." She was beginning to feel settled in this new belief system and it really felt good. Mason's eyes shone, and he seemed to understand exactly what she was thinking.

"Come here." She walked into his arms. "I think we got interrupted earlier when we were in the kitchen." She burst out laughing.

"We did not get interrupted. We were in the middle of a party doing inappropriate things."

"That's where you're wrong. Nothing we do is inappropriate." He drew her even closer, lifting her up so she was nestled against the ridge of his cock. She wiggled and he groaned. Reaching up, she touched those shoulders that beckoned, reveling in the hot strength. The man felt so good.

"I love the sounds you make when you get aroused." He was right, she was humming, but who wouldn't be? He had her in his arms and down the hall in record time.

He set her down beside the bed and she had her hands underneath his T-Shirt in a nano-second. "Lift up your arms." He did, but she soon saw it didn't help. He was too tall. "Take it off." He huffed out a laugh. As soon as the shirt was off it was like she had her own personal playground. The man was gorgeous.

"Now you."

"No, I want you naked and me dressed for a change."

He gave her a considering glance and nodded. He undressed and she grinned, pushing him down on to the bed. Of course it only worked because he allowed it. The man was covered in muscles and Sophia was determined to touch, lick, and kiss every one of them. Finally she'd touched everything but his cock and he was straining upwards, a fine sheen of sweat covering his body.

"You're killing me, honey."

"You're young, you can take it." She gently grasped his shaft.

"Do me a favor, I'm begging you."

"What?" she asked, unable to take her gaze away from his flesh.

"Take off your blouse. I want to see your breasts." Sophia looked at Mason's face, and saw he was serious. She pouted at having to stop touching him, but she did as he asked, throwing her blouse and bra over the side of the bed.

"You're staring."

"Well d'uh, you have these." He cupped her breasts in his hands and she arched up. Then he thumbed her nipples and she grabbed his wrists, trying to pull him away.

"No, it's my turn."

"Multi-task," she watched in wonder as his abdominal muscles rippled and he curled upwards to suck the tip of her breast in his mouth. His tanned, muscled shoulder was right there in front of her and she kissed and licked it. As he suckled harder she cried out and bit into his hard flesh.

Somehow she was on her back, and Mason was unzipping her shorts and pulling them off along with her panties. He had her legs over his arms and his hands on her ass, pulling her towards the edge of the bed where he was now kneeling. She had two seconds of brain cells left and she used them.

"I thought I got to multi-task."

"You do, you provide feedback so I know I'm doing things right." Smartass.

His thumbs parted her sex. At the first brush of his tongue all thought of providing feedback left her mind. Then Sophia lost all brainpower to the sensuous strokes that brought her right to the edge of climax.

"More, do you need more?" he teased as he crawled up onto the bed and caged her body.

Once again, she sighed with relief when she saw he was wearing a condom.

"Mason, now," she begged.

"Now what?"

"Oh God, we're doing the talking thing again?" she wailed.

"Specifics, honey. I respond well when I receive detailed orders." He was going to turn her brain to mush, and her body into a puddle of needy goo.

"I need your cock. I need it inside me. Now!"

Mason slid slowly inside her, filling her up, proving every single nerve in her body was connected to her core. But it wasn't enough. She didn't want slow, she didn't want gentle. She needed hard, she needed fast. His hands cupped her face, and his eyes were alight with laughter. The bastard knew.

Sophia turned her head and caught his thumb and sucked it into her mouth at the same time she tightened her inner muscles. She heard him gasp. She pushed up and kept up a rhythm.

"Oh…My…God." Apparently he liked it. She fluttered her tongue up and down his thick thumb, he surged deep and hard, and she moaned in pleasure. She turned her head wanting to look into his beautiful blue eyes. So much fun, so much pleasure, so much love, and she was so happy knowing he would see the same reflected in hers.

Just like that they went over into bliss together.

* * *

Mason wasn't all that surprised to find all the members of his team in his kitchen the next morning. He'd slept in. He'd known Clint was going to be there to discuss the findings from the night before last, but he wasn't surprised he called in the rest.

"I'm going to go kill the motherfuckers and be done with it," Drake said as he pulled out a coffee mug for Mason.

"It's a throwaway cell phone, we don't know for sure that it's the guys who tried to rape her," Mason growled.

"Doesn't matter. If the phone calls stop, it's a win. If the phone calls don't stop, it's still a win. It means we have to find the real caller is all." Damned if Drake didn't make it sound reasonable.

Darius slapped Drake in the back of the head…hard. Drake pulled out creamer from the fridge for him.

"How does Sophia want to handle her father?" Clint asked.

"What do you mean her father? I thought you said it was a throwaway cell phone?" Finn asked, clearly confused.

"It's worse than that. It could be an asshole from the diner," Mason said.

"Time-the-fuck-out. I need a fucking score card. We have 'would-be rapists', her father, and now some asshole from the diner. Someone better fucking tell me who I get to kill and tell me right quickly," Drake shouted.

"Keep you goddamn voice down," Mason damn near shouted back. "Sophia's still sleeping."

"Okay children, gather round and I shall explain using itty bitty little words so even Drake can understand," Clint said.

"Much appreciated." Drake nodded.

"All in all, Sophia has gotten over thirty-five calls from unidentified numbers. Twenty-one have come in mostly at night from a throw-away cell phone. This includes the call where the asshole talked to her and scared her. Eight have come in from various pay phones. The other six calls came from the unlisted number of her father's house in Mission Hills. Those six calls all came in during the work day. Sophia is thinking those came from her father's new wife."

"Okay, now I understand the father. Now breakdown who could be using the throwaway cell beside the fuckers from the alley," Drake demanded.

"Drake, you remember the other waitress who works at the diner?" Mason asked.

"The lazy one who hit on you?"

"That's her. Well her boyfriend tried to kiss Sophia and cop a feel and she kneed him in the nuts. So it could be him," Mason explained.

"What an asshole, it sounds like he and the assholes from the alley all need to be visited," Finn said.

"That's my thinking," Mason agreed. "Sophia wants to go over to her father's house today. I called the commander to get the next couple of days off, so we could get this shit figured out."

Finn coughed. Darius was grinning. Clint was looking into his coffee like it held the secrets of the universe and Drake started to laugh.

"What?" Mason frowned.

"We know," Drake said.

"What do you know?" Mason demanded.

"We know you took off time. We did too. Hell, except for Finn, nobody's taken off in a coon's age. The commander damn near kicked us off base."

Mason was overwhelmed as he looked at his friends.

"Oh Jesus, you're not going to cry, are you?" Drake demanded.

"Fuck you," Mason said without heat.

"So we divide and conquer?" Finn asked as he started to drink his coffee instead of just stare at it.

"Damn right," Drake said. "I want to conquer the fuck wads who are out on bail."

"Which is exactly why your ass is stuck with me and Sophia." Drake stopped laughing.

"Well don't be thinking you should put Clint in charge of the other team, he has his head up his ass about the girl from the jungle and…" Whatever else Drake was going to say was cut off as Clint's big hand wrapped around his throat. Drake stood there accepting the abuse, and realized he'd crossed a line.

"Easy Clint, you know his mouth engages before his brain does," Darius said. All the men watched as Clint slowly released Drake from his grip.

"I'm sorry dude, I should have known better." Clint gave a short nod. "So how is she doing? How is her family?"

"They're struggling. Some of the feds want to prosecute the dad, some want to put him in witness protection. In the meantime they're in a holding pattern and Lydia's still in the hospital."

"That doesn't make any sense she should be fine by now," Darius said.

Mason watched Clint. He was seeing signs of the frantic man in the jungle who thought the woman in his arms had died.

"She came in with a bad infection and then she ended up with pneumonia."

"They've actually let you see her? Where is she?" Drake asked.

"Texas. And no I'm not supposed to see her, and yes I have seen her." How had Mason not known about Clint taking a trip to Texas?

"And Drake, just to be clear, any day of the week I'm the better choice to lead the second team. Your ass would have us in jail, whereas I will definitely keep things under the radar."

"Yeah, like any of us can't pull off covert." Finn laughed, but then he immediately sobered. "Seriously Mase, what do you want us to do? I'm with Drake on this one. I want to plant them in the ground."

"First let's get some proof, okay? I want to know exactly what's been going on," Mason said.

"What about the asshat from the diner? Can I lead the team to go after him? We also need to make sure she stays safe. I know, going forward, you need to put a leash on her," Drake proclaimed.

"I beg your pardon?" And didn't that just figure? The worst possible thing coming out of Drake's mouth is when Sophia made her appearance.

"We were just talking about ways to keep you safe, after he explained about the asshole boyfriend at the diner. And before you give me shit Sophia, I didn't say he needed to spank you, because I figure this shit isn't your fault." All of the men groaned.

"Do you ever get laid?" Sophia asked as she headed towards the coffee maker. There was dead silence in the room. Mason looked around. Every man worked as hard as he was trying to keep their laughter inside and wait for Drake's reply. They didn't have to wait long.

"Yes, I get laid. I just have to keep to the flavors with the lower IQ's."

"How sad for you."

"It is." Drake said as he added creamer to the coffee he normally took black.

"How about some breakfast, guys?" Sophia asked after she took her first sip of coffee and eyed the men in the kitchen.

"That'd be great, but we'll help." Finn opened the refrigerator and started pulling out food. By the time breakfast was over, they had the outline of a plan. At least the basics of one they were willing to say in front of a civilian.

After they were done, Sophia looked around at each of them.

"I can't thank you enough. Knowing you are in my corner, means the world to me." His girl was learning.

Chapter Eighteen

"I hate that I'm so nervous."

Mason ran a soothing hand down her back as they stood outside the door of her father's house. Drake was lounging against the side of the truck, trying to look relaxed and nonchalant. He looked like a guard dog ready to attack. It actually made Sophia feel a little better having these two men at her back as she had to confront the man who belittled her throughout her life.

Mason rang the doorbell of the beautiful home. It was another thing that really bothered Sophia. He was living in such a nice house and he left his son in foster care? What kind of man was he?

They waited for what seemed like forever, and then finally they heard someone open the ornate peephole. The front door was quickly opened to reveal a young woman holding a toddler.

"Sophia, what are you doing here?" the woman asked.

Sophia stared. The woman looked almost identical to her mother when she had been young. It was beyond creepy. Sophia and Billy looked like their dad, their mom had been a brunette with blue eyes.

"Do I know you?" Sophia finally asked.

"I'm Ashley, your dad's wife. I saw you when you came here last year." The woman seemed really nervous. "Why are you here?" Ashley asked.

Sophia couldn't come up with a reply. The child started wiggling to be let down.

"Your dad's at work. Who is this?" she asked nodding to Mason.

"I'm Mason Gault, a friend of Sophia's."

"He's my boyfriend." What an innocuous term for the role Mason held in her life.

"Do you want to come in?"

"Sure, thanks."

They followed Ashley into the large sunlit living room and sat down on the couch she indicated.

"I don't understand. Why are you here?"

"Why have you been calling my phone?"

Ashley put down her daughter, who immediately tried to stand on her own, and then landed on her bottom. She giggled up at all of the adults in the room.

"This is Louisa," Ashley smiled down at the giggling baby, who was now crawling towards the coffee table. "She's the reason I wanted to talk to you. And I did mean to talk to you, but whenever I heard your voice, I lost my nerve and hung up." Ashley looked at Sophia with sad eyes. Immediately Sophia knew what was wrong.

"He's being mean to you, isn't he?"

Ashley twisted the large diamond ring on her finger around and around. She finally nodded. "He's been a bastard. For a while he actually had me believing it was me, until he started yelling at Louisa. She just turned two. When he comes into the room she starts to cry and it makes him yell even more."

"Oh Ashley." Sophia stared down at the beautiful brown haired little girl and just couldn't imagine anyone being mean to her. "What can I do for you? Do you need a place to stay? My apartment isn't big, but we can figure out something."

Ashley clapped a hand over her mouth and shook her head. Louisa crawled over to her, and lifted her arms clearly wanting up. Ashley picked her up and cuddled her.

"I'm all right, sweetheart," she assured the little girl. She looked at Sophia. "My God, he's been lying for years, hasn't he?"

"What do you mean?"

"I know about you. I know you work at the diner and live in the apartment over it. Here you are offering me a place to stay. Carl's been saying for years how Pam took him for everything and he had to start over. What selfish, ungrateful shits you and your brother were and that's why he cut you off. What kind of sociopath have I managed to marry?"

"Ashley, you and Louisa can come and stay with me for a bit until you get your bearings."

"I just needed confirmation it wasn't just me. That what I thought was real. He did this to you and your family too, right?"

"Oh yeah, he left when mom was in the middle of her cancer treatments. I was fifteen and Billy was five."

"That bastard," Ashley growled. Mason reached out and grabbed her hand. Ashley's tears dried up and she had a determined look on her face. "Sophia you offering to have me stay at your place has to be the sweetest thing ever. But my mom and dad have been trying to get me to come home for the last year, so I'm moving back in with them. Then I'm hiring the best divorce attorney in Southern California and taking him for everything he has."

"I don't get it. Why were you calling Sophia from the house line?" Mason asked.

"I knew it was unlisted, and my phone has my name pop up. How did you find out the calls were coming from this number?" Ashley looked from Sophia to Mason.

"Mason is a SEAL, his team members seem to have a lot of skills." Sophia laughed. Ashley joined in.

"A SEAL, huh. Well, as long as he's nothing like your dad, that's all that really matters." Sophia looked at the man beside her, then back at Ashley.

"He's the exact opposite. I couldn't have found anyone better."

Mason's grip on her hand tightened.

"Ashley, do you need any help packing?" Mason asked. Sophia watched as the other woman bit her lip.

"Would you mind waiting until my dad shows up? I'm going to call him, and I know he'll be here within the hour. I don't think Carl will come home until after work, but just in case, I don't want to be alone if he does, because I will probably lose my shit, ya know. I don't want to do that in front of Louisa"

"That's not a problem. Why don't you give him a call, and Sophia, why don't you get a ride back to your place with Drake?" Sophia looked at Mason and felt a sense of relief. She really didn't want any confrontations with the man who fathered her. Everyone stood up and Ashley came over and gave her a hug.

"Thank you so much for coming here. You gave me the information I needed to leave. We are so going to be keeping in touch. After all, you have a baby sister who is going to need you." Sophia looked at the girl on the floor and reeled at the thought. She hadn't even considered the fact until that very moment.

"I have a baby sister." She turned to Mason. "I have a baby sister! Isn't that great."

"And another thing, I'm going to make sure the rat bastard starts paying child support for Billy." Sophia just stared at Ashley, unable to believe what she was hearing.

"Can you do that?"

"Oh sweetie, with the right lawyer, you can do anything. Trust me, my daddy will make sure I have the best," she said with a grin.

"Are you sure you're the same woman who answered the door an hour ago?" Sophia asked.

"I'm not. But I remember who I was before I met and married Carl Anderson. I think with some time and distance I can get back to the girl I once was." Ashley turned to Mason. "I'm going to call my dad."

* * *

"Dooley sure as hell didn't do it," Finn said as he sat on Mason's picnic table. Mason listened, but most of his concentration was on Darius, who looked grim. He wanted to hear what Dare had to say, but knew he needed to wait for Finn to complete his report.

"Dooley damn near pissed himself when we showed up. The guy wants to take a plea so bad it's killing him. He babbled on about being in rehab. We couldn't get him to shut up." Clint nodded in agreement. Now that Finn was done talking, he looked over at Darius.

"Spill it Darius," Mason commanded. Darius continued to pace Mason's backyard. Even Drake was silent. Everyone watched him. Mason heard enough from Clint and Finn earlier to know it was Darius who talked to Krill, and he'd been on edge ever since.

"It's him. We need to do some recon," Darius bit out.

"What makes you so sure?" Mason asked.

"He denied it. He was smooth. He'll be good up in the witness stand. But his eyes were dead like a shark. He's a killer. You're not going to convince me this is his first time, he's been torturing animals since he was a kid." He stopped right in front of Mason, looking down at him where he sat.

"Psychopath," Drake said.

"With his sights set on Sophia," Darius concurred.

Mason controlled the urge to get to Sophia, but he needed to hear the rest.

"What about Brenda's boyfriend, Tate?"

"Oh, something's up with him," Clint said. "That dumbass was jumpy and mean, I wouldn't put it past him threatening your woman."

"Please note the past tense," Finn chimed in. "He won't be coming within fifty feet of her going forward." Mason looked between the three men and saw identical looks of satisfaction.

"I take it he now knows the fear of God?"

"Oh yes," Darius said with a satisfied smile. "It was nice being able to scare the bejesus out of him after having talked to Krill." That sobered Mason up.

"Of course, we can never discount the stupid factor, and our man Tate has that in spades."

"Fuck, there is that," Darius agreed.

"I'm going over to the diner right now," Mason said, getting up and pulling his keys out of his pocket. "She's working the lunch shift."

"We'll figure out a schedule, Mase. Your girl won't be left unprotected. You have our word on it," Darius assured him.

Mason felt the slightest bit of his tension ease knowing that every man on his team had Sophia's back. But he wasn't going to feel good until he was holding her safe in his arms.

Mason pushed the speed limit on the way to San Clemente. The diner was just closing as he arrived. He headed around the back so he could catch Peter.

"Hey Mason, Sophia's inside."

"I actually wanted to talk to you," Mason said to the older man.

"What's up?" Mason liked how Peter stopped on his way to his car, realizing something was wrong.

"A couple of guys on my team visited the bastards who beat up Sophia. We're convinced they're going to come after her before the trial. We're going to be here 24/7, but I wanted you to be aware." Peter's face went hard.

"I might never have been in the armed services, but I know how to protect the people I love. Make no mistake, I consider Margie and Sophia my family. I'll help any way I can." Mason felt even more tension roll off his shoulders.

"Thanks, Pete. I better get inside." Mason went in the backdoor and heard Brenda's raised voice.

"I'm just saying you need to stay away from him. He doesn't appreciate you trying to get into his pants."

Fuck, this was definitely the day from hell.

"Brenda, I want Tate like I want a hole-in-the-head. I didn't want to tell you this, but he's come onto me. I don't think he's been faithful to you." The last was said with empathy. God, Sophia was too nice for her own good. Mason walked into the dining room.

"Mason, your girlfriend is trying to cheat on you with my boyfriend. You better keep a close eye on her," Brenda said. Mason cringed, her voice sounded like nails on a chalkboard. He walked up to Sophia and put his arm around her waist.

"You're out of your mind, Brenda. Tate is the one who has come onto me and I had to beat him off. If anyone better keep a close eye on their lover, it's you."

"I trust Sophia. Isn't it time for you to leave?" She gave the two of them a dark look, and rushed to the kitchen. She was back with her purse, and left without a backward glance.

"So, it seems like you were having a good day. I was surprised when you called me and said you were going to work today. I thought you said Margie was taking care of the diner."

"Helen wasn't feeling well so she wanted to babysit again. I said I could cover." Mason dropped a kiss on her forehead. Of course Sophia was going to cover for Margie.

"So when are you going to fire Brenda and hire some *real* help?"

"You're a mind reader. Margie and I were talking about that. She put the word out the other day. She's hoping to have some applicants soon. I want to know why you're here. I thought I wouldn't see you until tomorrow."

"How about I take you out to dinner? Maybe have a margarita or two?" Her face lit up.

"That would be great. Ashley called me, I can fill you in on that. I didn't realize her mom and dad are rich. Her dad actually has a lawyer on retainer and everything. So she wasn't kidding about having the best divorce attorney in Southern California," Sophia giggled. "My dad isn't going to know what hit him."

Mason smiled as he guided her up the stairs to her apartment. He waited while she changed. He got a charge out of the fact Ashley already texted her with pictures of Louisa. Of course Sophia was over the moon.

* * *

Sophia knew it had to be bad if Mason was stalling.

"Mason, I can handle whatever you need to tell me," she said as she reached across the table and grabbed his hand. Mason looked at her and smiled. He turned his hand over and laced their fingers.

"I know, you're the strongest person I've ever met, honey." Sophia snorted.

"Seriously, Sophia. What you've been through would have broken most people, but you just keep getting up and taking care of business."

"For just a moment, let's also call things out, okay? I totally suffer from self-esteem issues. I am constantly worried I'm not good enough. Hell, I get on my own nerves half the time. I still have a lot of things I need to work on."

He rubbed his thumb over her knuckles and looked into her eyes and smiled.

"Okay, maybe a little bit," he acknowledged. "But I love every part of you, even the parts that need a little extra care and feeding. What the fuck, you even put up with me when I channel Drake Avery." She burst out laughing. Thank God, she hadn't been eating.

"Good point. Now tell me what you haven't wanted to tell me." She stopped at his grimace, but continued. "Is it really that bad?" Now she began to regret having eaten so much.

"I wasn't there. You know it was Darius, Clint, and Finn who went and met with…"

"I know," Sophia cut him off, not wanting to hear their names.

"Anyway, Darius is sure you're right. That one is behind the calls and it's not safe for you. I wanted you to move in with me, but it's not practical with you needing to be at the diner so early in the morning."

"I'm not surprised that was your first thought." Mason protects people, that's who he was.

"Yes it was. So instead I'm proposing that I move in with you, until this is over with."

Her knee jerk reaction was to say no, that she could handle this on her own. But looking into the eyes of the man she loved, the man she knew she could depend on…

"I would feel a lot safer if you moved in," she finally admitted.

Mason let out a deep breath.

"Thank God."

"I take it you didn't think I would go for it?" Despite the scary situation, she was happy that she surprised Mason in a good way.

Mason brought her hand to his lips and kissed her fingers.

"I was worried. But there's more. When I can't be here, one of the team is going to be here with you."

"Isn't that overkill?" Sophia couldn't help the feeling of dread in the pit of her stomach.

"I'm sorry honey, but Krill has Darius really worried."

"How long?"

"Until the trial." His gaze was calm and steady.

"But that's five weeks away."

"They know that. It's not a problem."

She saw he was dead serious.

"Look Mason, I can handle you living with me, that makes sense, but all of the others being here, it's too much." She wrenched her hand out of his.

"Sophia, it's not a big deal."

"Are you out of your mind? Of course it's a big deal. You're saying for the next five weeks, if not you, then one of your team is going to be by my side, correct?" He nodded slowly.

"That's a big fucking deal," she whispered furiously.

He winced. She didn't use the "F" word all that much so he must know she was upset.

"Yeah it is. But every one of them volunteered. You can't keep them away. They're not doing it for me, they're doing it for you." His calm voice didn't make her feel any better.

"They're going to put their lives on hold because of me?" It was too much to take in. She fumbled in her purse for some cash and placed it on the table. "Let's go."

Mason frowned at her paying but had the good sense not to argue.

She walked to his truck and waited while he opened her door and helped her in. The process settled them both. When he got in, he once again proved he understood her, because he asked where she'd like to go, instead of just assuming she wanted to go home.

"Moonlight Beach." It seemed fitting since it's where she'd first seen him. They were silent during the drive. He magically had the same thick coat in the backseat to keep her warm.

"What were you? An Eagle Scout?" she asked as he helped her slip it on, before heading down to the shore.

"The Navy teaches you to be prepared. I always want to make sure I'm taking care of you." The man had the most beautiful eyes. She stroked his jaw and he arched into the caress.

"I love you, Mason, even when you make me crazy. I love you." He took her hand and they strolled down to the beach. When they got there and sat down, she snuggled into his arms and looked at the blue and pink sunset sky.

"So explain it to me. Explain why you can finally lean on me, but you can't let my friends take care of you too."

She heard the confusion in his voice. She tried to twist around so she could see his face, but he kept her between his knees, facing forward, his head resting on hers.

It took Sophia a while to answer. "I love you Mason, and I trust you. I finally believe you when you said you won't think of me as a burden when I need your support. That you'll still love and respect me when I need to lean on you. I just don't have that level of trust with your friends. To make it worse, I'm afraid that they'll think badly of you for having a girlfriend that requires so much time and effort." His arms pulled her closer to his chest.

"I feel like I've won a medal."

"For having the most neurotic girlfriend," she teased ruefully.

"Shit Sophia, do you realize what a big deal it is for you to have agreed for me to stay at your place? It's huge. And the reason for the medal, is that you chose me." He nuzzled her neck, and they stayed like that for long minutes, watching as the sky changed colors.

"Okay medal boy. You still want to tell me that I need to let the others watch after to me?"

"You've got it in one." This time when she tried to turn around to look at him, he let her.

"It's just so much to ask."

"But you're not asking. This is what we do. They're an extension of me. They're my team, my brothers. After having worked as a unit for so long together, we can't *not* come together in our personal lives. Sophia, you *are* my personal life. I love you."

It was amazing that she could still feel her heart beat since it was so much goo it must be actually oozing out of her chest.

"I love you too Mason. All right, I can accept this help. When I start getting antsy, and I will, can you give me a shake?"

"How about if I kiss you out of your antsiness?"

"That'll work." Their lips met, and she melted even more. When they let up for air, she giggled.

"What?" he asked.

"So what crazy plan do you and your friends have cooked up?"

"Well, besides loving you…like a sister…they all want free food. I have a list in my truck. Clint wants apple brown betty."

"That would be Darius," she corrected.

"Whatever. Just know they aren't doing this for free. I of course want sexual favors." Just like that he managed to make a stressful situation fun.

"What about your work? What happens if you have to go on a mission?"

"I've already talked to my commander. I've explained the situation. Until the trial I'm stateside. I explained it was a family emergency. He understands."

Sophia thought she might melt again at him using the term family.

"I need to explain to Billy why he can't come over for a while. I don't want him in harm's way." Mason kissed her temple.

"I think that's probably for the best."

They sat like that until the sun went down. Then Mason took her back to her apartment and they made love until she finally fell asleep without any nightmares.

CHAPTER NINETEEN

With only a couple of exceptions, the last three weeks were the happiest of Mason's life. The only thing that could make it better, is if Sophia were living in his house, but he intended to take care of that after the trial. Every night he was in her bed, and he had the added bonus of having all of his friends thinking he was the luckiest bastard on the face of the planet.

They'd reported the phone calls to the police and the D.A., but as expected, there wasn't a lot that could be done. They found the same thing—the calls came from a throwaway phone. Clint blocked the number from coming into Sophia's phone. Then another unidentified number started calling. Drake was there when that happy horse shit started, and he'd been so angry Sophia was lucky her phone was still in one piece. Clint blocked that number as well.

Finn took a week to go to Minnesota to help his mother move to San Diego. Clint was still tied up in knots over Lydia, but at least she was now out of the hospital. But according to her sister, Elsbeth, she was bedridden.

The trial was set for mid-August and he had talked his parents into coming down to stay with him for the first of November. He really wanted them to meet Sophia and Billy. He was on the way into the base after having spent the night at Sophia's apartment. He'd left with Clint eating a big enough breakfast for two people. He was still in paperwork hell. He hit the speaker on his phone.

"Drake, I'm going to need your help today."

"Name a day when you don't need my help."

Mason laughed.

"Seriously, you have sisters, one of them is even married. I need taste and judgment."

"You're going ring shopping and you're asking me? You're a dumb shit." Drake's disgust carried clearly through the phone. "Mase, you need to ask Margie and Frannie. I can't believe I even have to tell you this."

Mason wanted to hit his forehead against the steering wheel but commuter traffic on the Five Freeway was hell.

"Okay, I will gladly accept the dumb shit award."

"How is Sophia doing? She seemed antsy yesterday."

"She wants the trial to be over. I want the trial to be over. On the good news front. Her dad is rolling over on the divorce. Ashley hired a private investigator. Apparently he'd been playing fast and loose with his company expense reports. So she is holding that over his head. He's even agreeing to pay back child support for Billy. Ashley is ruthless. I really like her."

Drake was laughing midway through his story.

"That is a beautiful thing. I'll invite Ashley to the next big food fest at your house. I talked to Tony, he said as long as we covered the booze he could talk the ladies into cooking. Apparently they like cooking for studs like us."

"How about Tony, what's his incentive?"

"Happy wife, happy life. Frannie really enjoyed herself, and having her happy worked out well for him. So he's more than happy to cook."

"I'll coordinate one for this coming weekend since I'm going to be talking to Frannie and Margie today."

"Great, I'll tell Ashley," Drake drawled.

"Excuse me? Did I just hear you say you're going to call Ashley Crandall? Sophia's soon to be ex-stepmother?" That sure as hell came from left field. There was silence on the phone.

"When you had me drive Sophia home that day from her dad's house, all she did was talk about Ashley and Louisa. She said she was worried her dad could end up trying to intimidate her. I offered to call her. Sophia really liked the idea."

"So how often have you called her?"

"Well I've met her a couple of times. I just wanted to make sure she was all right, and knew she had someone she could reach out to if she needed protection." Mason thought about the pretty brunette. He could easily see how Drake might be attracted, but still.

"She is just coming out of a shitty relationship and she's still married."

"I know that. It's nothing like that. She just reminds me of one of my sisters."

"Yeah, sure."

"Look asshole, I'm just saying I can call and invite her over to the food fest is all." Mason decided to let it drop.

"Sounds good to me."

* * *

"I don't like Brenda."

Sophia laughed at Clint's dark expression. She'd taken a seat in the opposite side of him in the booth. He'd been watching the whole breakfast rush, and it had finally dwindled down to nothing, and she had time to rest.

"Better not let her hear that or she might spit in your food."

"Nah, you always serve me." Clint smiled. Sophia was happy to see he was now drinking tea instead of coffee. These men drank far too much coffee as far as she was concerned.

"Why don't you fire her?"

"Keep your voice down."

"It is down." He was right nobody could hear him. Come to think of it, all of Mason's team mates knew how to whisper. Well, except for Drake, he seemed to only know how to yell.

"Margie and I have found a perfect replacement but she can't start for two weeks. She's doing the responsible thing and put in her notice. I really like her."

"That's great. Brenda's a lazy skank."

Sophia laughed at the disgust in Clint's voice.

"I sure don't ever want to get on your bad side."

"You never could. Even if you broke up with Mason, I would still think highly of you. You're a good person."

Sophia stared into Clint's sincere eyes. It was amazing how her entire self-assessment had been put on its ear since meeting Mason.

"Thank you, I think you're pretty wonderful too. As a matter of fact, I made some cherry pie this morning." His face broke out in a grin, his hazel eyes twinkling.

"Did I say good person? You're a goddess!" Sophia looked up as the door tinkled, and saw six people coming in.

"Oops, looks like some early customers for lunch. I'd better get a move on."

Sophia looked around for Brenda but she was nowhere to be found. After thirty minutes of handling the customers on her own, she went out back and saw Brenda and Tate smoking cigarettes and talking.

"Brenda, I need you to help me, the lunch rush is starting."

"She's taking her break." Tate sneered.

"Brenda, you've already had a break and your lunch break," Sophia said, ignoring Tate.

"I'll be there in a few."

"I need you now."

"I said I would be there when I'll be there."

Sophia mentally counted to ten.

"Brenda if you don't come in now, you're fired."

"You can't fire me. Who else is going to work at this shit-hole?"

"I'll find someone. Are you coming in or not?"

"Fine." She threw her cigarette on the ground and stomped it out.

Sophia held the door open for her and Brenda flounced in. Before Sophia could follow, Tate grabbed her shoulder.

"I was talking to her and it was important."

"So is her job."

"You think you're so high and mighty. You're nothing."

"Get your hands off of her." Clint picked Tate up like he weighed nothing and Tate was on his back on the parking lot. "Sophia, you need to tell me if you're going anyplace other than the bathroom or the kitchen, remember?"

"You whore. Are you sleeping your way through the whole army?"

"The Navy. I'm sleeping my way through the whole Navy. Get it right." She turned to Clint. "Thanks. I've got to get back inside. Can you come with me?" She really didn't want Clint wasting anymore of his time on this piss ant.

"Bowers, you weren't supposed to be coming around the diner anymore. Expect a visit tonight." Clint glared at the man on the ground and then turned back to Sophia.

"What was that about?" Sophia asked.

"Nothing."

Sophia watched as Tate ran towards his car like the hounds of hell were chasing him.

Before the day was over Sophia wasn't at all surprised to find Clint in back helping Peter with all the dishes. Usually all of Mason's men couldn't stay still in the diner, they had to be doing something, and they all ended up doing KP. Peter loved this new program.

Her phone rang and she was happy to see it was Mason.

"I'm on my way."

"Well then, I'll get the cherry pie and brownies with ice cream ready."

"Oh yeah, it's Clint who's there today. For some reason I thought it was Darius."

"Good for you. You're remembering who likes what desserts. I'm so proud of you," Sophia teased.

"I'm bringing your favorite dessert for you."

"Yum, I love Almond Joy." Out of the corner of her eye she saw Brenda yelling into her cell phone. She walked past where Sophia was sitting and she heard her telling Tate to go to hell, and that they were through. Apparently their time in paradise was over. At least for today.

"What was that?" Mason asked.

"Nothing, just the usual. I'll see you soon." She hung up and then her phone rang again.

"Did you forget something?"

"No I remembered everything."

Sophia slammed down her phone. Fuck! She'd thought since Clint had blocked the last number she was done getting these calls. Her hand was trembling.

"What? Trouble in paradise?" Brenda asked, echoing her earlier thoughts.

"Isn't it time for you to leave?" Sophia asked.

"You have to pay me."

Sophia got up from the booth and made her way back to the desk in the kitchen.

"So is your SEAL finally kicking you to the curb?" Brenda asked as they went through the swinging door. Clint and Peter looked at one another and Sophia ignored her.

"Just take your paycheck and leave." Sophia handed Brenda an envelope.

Brenda grabbed it and stormed out of the kitchen. When the bell over the front door rang all three of them sighed in relief.

"That bitch is twisted," Clint said.

"Her last day can't come soon enough," Peter agreed.

Clint's phone rang. He flicked the water off his hands, grabbed a towel, and then pulled his phone out of his pocket and answered it. Immediately Sophia could tell it was bad news.

"Is everything all right?" Sophia asked after he hung up.

"I need to catch the next flight to Dallas." He was looking at his phone, obviously searching for reservations. Within five minutes he was on the phone.

"Mason, it's Clint. I have a situation. Lydia is back in the hospital. I can't stand the thought of her going through another bout of pneumonia without me again. I can catch a flight out of Orange County if I leave now."

Sophia watched as he listened intently.

"Yep, Peter's here. Great, you'll be here in twenty? Okay, I'll have them lock up behind me."

As soon as Clint hung up she went up to him and gave him a strong hug. "I'll say a prayer for her. Please call and let me know how she's doing, okay?"

He nodded, his eyes anguished. He turned to Peter.

"Don't worry, son, I've got this. Go take care of your lady." Clint shook Peter's hand and they followed him to the back door and locked it after he left.

They went back into the kitchen to finish the cleanup.

"So who is this Lydia?" Peter asked.

"I haven't really asked, but from what I've gathered, they rescued her on their last mission. She was badly injured and Clint carried her for days to safety."

"Well I hope she's all right. I know when Ruth was sick I was a basket case."

"I remember," Sophia teased. "She just had a head cold."

"But you made her a pineapple upside down cake, which is her favorite, and brought it over to her. She still talks about that. You're a good girl."

Sophia blushed. They looked up from the sink when there was a sound at the back door.

"Clint must have forgotten something," Peter said.

"I'll go." Sophia grabbed a towel. The door from the back opened and there stood her attacker from the alley holding a gun.

"I knew your watchdogs would eventually leave you alone. I just needed patience. I've finally gotcha, girly." He smiled. Out of the corner of her eye she saw Peter pick up one of the knives out of the dishwater. As Krill moved closer, Peter lunged, and a shot rang out.

Sophia screamed as she saw Peter lying on the floor blood pouring from his chest.

"Stop screaming!" He was standing right in front of her. She could smell his breath, see his eyes.

Dead eyes. She was going to die. Oh God, she was going to die. He hit her and everything went black.

* * *

"Peter?" Mason recognized the number, but all he heard was heavy breathing. "Peter? Answer me man." Still nothing. Mason was still fifteen minutes away from the diner. "Peter?"

"Shot. Took Sophia."

Ah fuck. No.

"You're shot and someone took Sophia?" *Say he got it wrong.*

"Yes." It was just a gasp of air.

"Hang on Peter, I'm getting you help. You did good man." Mason hung up the phone and dialed 911.

Thirteen minutes away.

Twelve minutes away.

"No, I won't stay on the phone. Get to Omega Grill in San Clemente. A man has been shot." Mason hung up the phone.

He voice dialed Drake.

Ten minutes away.

"Pete's been shot, Sophia's been taken."

"Where the fuck is Clint?" Drake demanded.

"On his way to the Orange County Airport, Lydia's sick."

"He's closest, I'm calling him back. The rest of us will be at the diner as soon as we can."

Six minutes away.

Finally he was there. Cop cars were everywhere. He pulled up next to Sophia's baby blue Cadillac. Peter was being loaded into the ambulance. He rushed up to talk to him, pushing past the officers who tried to stop him.

"I'm family," Mason said.

Peter shoved off the oxygen mask.

"Son," he gasped out. He couldn't be doing too badly if he could play along with Mason.

Mason bent down close to Peter. "Do you know where he took Sophia?"

"No. He knocked her unconscious and dragged her out of the diner. I didn't tell the cops. I knew you boys would be the best ones to find her." Mason replaced the mask over Peter's mouth.

"Take care of my dad," he told the EMT as Clint came running towards him.

"Mason, what…"

"Not here." Mason grabbed his arm and led him away from the ambulance and the prying eyes of the police. He pulled him towards his truck.

Mason's phone rang. It was Drake. "Clint there?"

"Yep."

"Good, he was the closest. The rest of us will be there between five and forty minutes depending on where we were when we got the call." Mason looked at Clint. There was no conflict on his face. He was there and ready for action. He had his laptop out and was doing something.

"Mase, are you keeping it together?" Drake asked.

"Yes."

"He took her, he didn't kill her. That's good news," Drake said, stating the obvious, but it made Mason want to cry, throw up, or kill his friend.

"Gotta go." Mason hung up.

Clint had his computer booted up and was keying in something Mason had no chance of comprehending.

"Good, her cell phone is on. I've got a GPS signal."

"Where is she?"

"She's heading north on Pacific Coast Highway." They looked at each other. It was good news she was moving. Krill had plans for her. All she had to do was survive until they got there.

"Can you arrange for my cell phone to track her cell phone?"

"Hand it over." Mason gave it to Clint. The man was amazing. After he was done he did the same thing with his phone.

They got in Mason's truck and Mason took the Five Freeway to Newport Beach, and then turned west towards PCH. Clint used Mason's phone to keep track of the signal and used his phone to inform the team of their whereabouts.

"Faster, they've stopped," Clint said urgently.

"Where are they?"

"Costa Mesa."

Clint gave Mason directions. They pulled up to a very small storage unit. The gates were closed. Mason gave a grim smile when he saw the chain and padlock. He went into the back of his truck and pulled out the industrial sized wire cutters and easily cut the chain.

The yard was small and not wanting to alert Krill, they ran instead of taking the truck. In less than a minute they saw a white minivan parked outside one of the units. Krill had the storage door open. The inside of the unit was eerily empty.

Mason motioned for Clint to come around from the back side. He waited a minute for him to get into position. Then he called out.

"Hey asshole, remember me?"

Krill stilled. He squinted into the sunlight trying to make out Mason's features. Then he calmly opened the sliding door to the minivan and Mason started at a dead run towards him. Clint was running quietly towards the other side of the vehicle.

When Mason got there, Krill had a broken beer bottle against Sophia's neck and she was awake.

"It's almost perfect. I thought about getting a knife but I wanted to replay the night exactly. Too bad Dooley's not here."

Mason shuddered. The man was evil.

"Let her go."

"All I have to do is press in. This is right at her jugular. She was supposed to be some fun the last time, and then die. Now she'll die and quit causing me so many problems."

Mason could see Clint at the open driver's side window.

"If you kill her you'll never see the inside of a prison."

"Seeing her dead first will be worth it."

Mason gave an imperceptible nod and Clint took his shot. Sophia started screaming as she was splattered with blood, and Mason jumped in and pulled her out of the van.

"Sophia, I have you baby." She kept screaming and thrashing. Mason had to hold her and repeat himself a couple more times. Abruptly she stopped.

"Mason? Oh God, Mason!" She sank into his arms. Then she started to cry and clear off the splatter from her face. He yanked off his shirt and wiped all the gore he could.

"Oh baby, I'm so sorry this happened. I have you. You're safe now. I'm so sorry. You're safe. I love you so much."

She shivered and clung to him. She looked up at him as he cleaned her face like he would a child. He pulled her into his lap and cradled her head to his chest and just let her cry.

"I was so scared but I always knew you'd come. I never doubted it for one moment." Something settled inside of him.

"I'll always come for you Sophia. I'd die if something happened to you. You're my world."

EPILOGUE

Four Months Later…

"Get a move on Billy, we're going to be late."

The door to her brother's bedroom flew open and he had a backpack slung over one arm and his wetsuit over his other. She winced as she saw the state of his bedroom. Part of her thought she should get on his case to clean it, but she was just too happy having them living together to sweat the small stuff.

"I saw that." Billy grinned at her.

"What?" she asked innocently. "The fact I'm considering calling the Hoarders TV Show?"

"I'll clean it when we get back from Mase's house on Monday, I promise." Sophia smiled. When Billy Anderson made a promise, he kept it.

"Thanks, I appreciate it."

"Come on, we don't want to be late. I can't wait to meet Mase's parents."

"I'm going to need help loading the car with the desserts," Sophia said as she headed to their new apartment's kitchen.

"Already done, Soph. While you took a zillion hours primping, I loaded my surfboard and the mountain of desserts you baked. You look awesome. Mase's tongue is going to be hanging out."

Sophia blushed. She was wearing a new yellow halter summer dress with red heels. Ever since she started going to counseling she found she could sleep and eat, so she filled out the dress a little bit better.

"Thanks, I needed to hear that."

"So let's go. Tonight we eat and tomorrow we surf. It's a perfect weekend." Sophia grabbed her overnight bag and looked over the apartment before locking the door. She still couldn't believe it belonged to her. Thank God for Ashley's lawyer. He'd made her dad start paying child support for Billy so they could afford a new place, and she was going to start taking college courses again. Everything was turned off, and she shut off the last light, and then closed and locked the door.

Yippee! She got to go to Mason's house for the weekend. She was more excited than Billy.

* * *

"You know my birthday is the day after Halloween."

"I know, Mom. Ever since I was fourteen I've never forgotten your birthday," Mason said as he hugged his petite mother.

"Let's never speak of the day again." They both laughed. He was so happy having his parents, Billy, and Sophia in his house for this first weekend in November. He looked over to where Sophia was helping Tony with his eggplant parmigiana.

"Mason, you're not paying attention."

"What Mom?"

"I said I know what I want you to get me for my birthday this year."

"Okay. But I already bought your gift."

"Well return it. I want a daughter."

"You just met Sophia today, how do you know you want her as a daughter-in-law?" His mother pulled him out of the kitchen, through the crowded living room, and onto the front porch.

"Mason, let's be serious for a moment. I have never seen you happier in your life. I know how much your career means to you. It has given you a wealth of satisfaction. I couldn't have been more proud. But listening to you on the phone for the last few months has warmed my heart. You are head over heels in love with this girl, and everything you've told me about her is true. She is such a good person and she is just like me."

"What do you mean by that?" Mason asked, really curious. He loved his mom to death but she could be a bulldozer. He didn't see where Sophia was a lot like her.

"Sophia thinks the sun revolves around you the same as I do." Mason's heart clenched as he saw his mom's eyes water.

"You got it wrong. I know I'm the lucky one because I have the two best girls in the world who love me."

"Sweet talker. You get that from your dad." He hugged his mom, so happy she and his dad were here for this special occasion.

"So do you have the ring?" She gave him a knowing grin.

"You're sure I'm going to propose today?"

"I didn't raise a stupid man."

Mason laughed.

"No, you didn't. Sophia is the best thing that's ever happened to me, and I'm going to do my damnedest to make sure she's by my side for the next fifty years." Mason gripped the ring box in his pocket and swallowed hard. Today truly was the first day of the rest of his life. They went inside and he was in time to take a huge bowl of macaroni salad out of Sophia's hands.

"I've got that, honey. Why don't you go out and grab a seat next to Peter and Ruth." Sophia smiled at him and then grinned at his mom.

"Have you met Peter and his wife, Linnie?"

"No, but I want to. How's he doing?" Mason watched as they proceeded him out the kitchen door. It was great to see how comfortable Sophia was with his mom, considering how worried she'd been to meet her. He stopped for a moment as the kitchen door shut behind him. His backyard was filled to the brim with his friends and family.

"Quit dawdling. People won't start eating until the host sits down and I'm hungry," Drake yelled.

Mason laughed. He went and sat next to Sophia who leaned into him. He couldn't wait for tonight. Drake winked at him. Clint gave him a nod. Everything was going to be in place.

* * *

Big warm hands caressed her back and Sophia arched into Mason's body. The man's touch was magic and she couldn't get close enough to him.

"Are you awake, honey?"

"Oh yeah," she whispered against his neck breathing him in. God, he smelled good. Her hands roamed downwards, but he caught them and brought them to his mouth, and kissed her palms.

"I have a surprise for you."

She wiggled closer and felt his surprise rising against her lower body.

"Not that," he admonished. "I need you to get up and get dressed.

"Huh?" She glanced over at the clock on the nightstand. It was two thirty in the morning.

"No questions," he gave her a slow and soft Mason kiss. She would now do anything he asked. "Up woman, get dressed."

She grinned. She put on a jeans and a hoodie, and took a moment to admire Mason pulling on clothes. The man was sex on a stick, and he was hers!

"Come on time's a wastin'." She gave a brief thought to Billy and then remembered Linnie and Fred were staying in the house. So all was good. Mason had them in his truck in no time. She didn't ask any questions as they headed towards the ocean. It didn't come as a shock the beach was their destination. She figured they were headed to Moonlight Beach, but when he passed it, she started to get curious.

She shot him a sideways look and he grinned. This was so cool. With her having custody of Billy they didn't get a chance to be on their own very much anymore. So she was soaking up this adventure. Mason pulled up to an area that was a private beach clearly owned by some of the expensive homes nearby. Again she looked at him.

"A surprise, remember?" He helped her out of the truck and she saw some lights up ahead. As they got closer to the path to the beach she saw on either side there were candles lighting the way towards a canopy covered blanket.

"Mason, what?" He pulled her into his arms and gave her a long slow kiss.

"No questions." He held her hand, and they followed the lit path towards the blanket. When they got there, she saw it was her pink blanket and she stared down at it in wonder. The entire canopy was surrounded by tea light candles. Mason helped her step over them and they stood in the center and she looked at him.

"I don't understand."

"It's simple. You're my world."

She watched as he got down on one knee, and the world stopped. All she could hear was the ocean and her heartbeat. He pulled a small box out of his pocket. He opened it up, and inside was a ring that shined.

She sank to her knees.

"You are my everything. My hero."

"So you'll marry me? You'll be mine for the rest of our days?"

"Yes, a million times yes." She flung her arms around his neck and he held her close. Through her tears, she could see the vast ocean and realized every one of her big dreams had come true.

THE END

If you enjoyed this book, or any book, please consider leaving a review. It's appreciated by authors more than you know. Thank You! Caitlyn

About the Author

Caitlyn O'Leary is an avid reader, and considers herself a fan first and an author second. She reads a wide variety of genres, but finds herself going back to happily-ever-afters. Getting a chance to write, after years in corporate America, is a dream come true. She hopes her stories provide the kind of entertainment and escape she has found from some of her favorite authors.

Keep up with Caitlyn O'Leary:

Facebook: http://tinyurl.com/nuhvey2
Twitter: http://twitter.com/CaitlynOLearyNA
Pinterest: http://tinyurl.com/q36uohc
Goodreads: http://tinyurl.com/nqy66h7
Website: http://www.caitlynoleary.com
Email: caitlyn@caitlynoleary.com
Newsletter: http://bit.ly/1WIhRup
Instagram: http://bit.ly/29WaNIh

Books by Caitlyn O'Leary

The Sisters Series

Tempting Fire, Book One (*Sisters Series and Dallas Fire &*
Rescue Crossover Novel; Paige Tyler KindleWorld)

Fate Harbor Series Published by Siren/Bookstrand
Trusting Chance, Book One
Protecting Olivia, Book Two
Claiming Kara, Book Three
Isabella's Submission, Book Four
Cherishing Brianna, Book Five